LEON CAZADOR, P.I.

Nik Morton

Collected short stories – Volume 6

(Detective fiction)

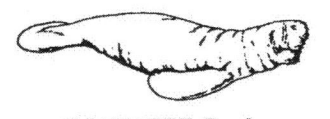

MANATEE *Books*

Nik Morton

LEON CAZADOR, P.I.

*Leon Cazador holds back
the encroaching night of unreason*

Private Investigator Leon Cazador is half-English, half-Spanish and wholly against the ungodly.

In these fascinating fiction stories, based on real events, we glean an insight into Cazador's past and the people he has rubbed shoulders with: his connections run wide and deep, which is to be expected of a man who served in the Spanish Foreign Legion, liaised with Japanese police, and was a spy in Afghanistan, the Gulf, China and Yugoslavia.

In his adventurous life he has witnessed many travesties of justice so, when he finally goes private, he uses his considerable skills to right wrongs.

Cazador translated into English means *hunter*. He is a man driven to hunt down felons of all kinds, to redress the balance of good against evil.

Sometimes, Cazador operates in disguise under several aliases, among them Carlos Ortiz Santos, a modern day Simon Templar, and tries to hold back the encroaching night of unreason.

He combats drug-traffickers, grave robbers, al-Qaeda infiltrators, misguided terrorists and conmen. Dodgy Spanish developers and shady expat English face his wrath. Traders in human beings, stolen vehicles and endangered species meet their match. Kidnappers, crooked mayors and conniving Lotharios come within his orbit of ire. Vengeful Chinese and indebted Japanese are his friends – and his enemies.

Leon Cazador fights injustice in all its forms and often metes out his own rough justice. It's what he does.

Nik Morton

LEON CAZADOR, P.I.

Collected short stories – Volume 6

The right of Nik Morton to be identified as the Author of the Work has been asserted by him in accordance with the Copyright, Designs and Patents Act 1988.

ALL RIGHTS RESERVED
No part of this book may be reproduced or transmitted in any form or by any means, electronic or mechanical, including photocopying, recording, or by any information storage and retrieval system, without written permission of the author or Manatee Books except for brief quotations used for promotion or in reviews.

This is a work of fiction.
Names, characters, places, and incidents are used fictitiously. Any resemblance to actual persons living or dead, business establishments, events, or locales, is entirely coincidental.

Manatee Books

Previously published as
Spanish Eye 2010 & 2013
now with the added story 'Processionary Penitents'

Republished with an extra story by Manatee Books
This collection © 2017 Nik Morton

ISBN-13: 978-1978401129
ISBN-10: 1978401124

Cover image:
Dreamstime image #25218461

Leon Cazador, P.I.

Some reviews of the previous published versions:

… In his crisp depiction of Leon Cazador, Nik Morton paints a portrait of everyone's hero. This cross-cultural character is dashing, daring, and delightful. He does whatever it takes to make good triumph over evil. While reading these exciting stories I experienced myriad emotions. I laughed, cried, and became incensed. I cheered and clapped, but most of all I felt a confirmation of universal values. - E.B. Sullivan, author of *Different Hearts*

… His voice is so unique, and his stories are as thought-provoking as they are entertaining. There are beautiful moments in the prose that never get purple or fluffy. He masters the art of taking an adventure and condensing it into short shots. If you enjoy short stories, you'll love this collection featuring the same character and exotic settings. - D. Thorne, editor

… a collection of short stories set in the heat and the dust of Spain.… These stories are humorous, insightful and sometimes tragic. Leon Cazador is not afraid to bring the bad men to justice, and so help to restore the balance in this world. Beautifully written with a simple and uncluttered style which draws you in to the heart of the story. Highly recommended! - Laura Graham, actress, author of *Down a Tuscan Alley*

This collection of detective stories is a really great read. Linked together by the main character Leon Cazador there is a wide variety of complex cases, some of them take you back to detectives such as The Saint. Beautifully written by someone who obviously knows how to tell a story it's the perfect kind of book to read in your spare moments or get sucked into on holiday. Fantastic stuff!
– Amazon reviewer

… The tales run the gamut of the usual crime stories (con men, kidnappings, car theft ring, crooked politicians) and the odd stuff (terrorists, smuggling exotic animals and illegal aliens). All fun stories, a bit of humour here and there, others deadly serious. One story had me grinning at the beginning, but sobering quickly as the end approached. Leon Cazador is not your typical P.I. - George R Johnson, reviewer

Morton has used his storytelling skills to ultimate effect. Leon Cazador offers not only the experience of righting wrongs and helping society become a safer place, he also spends time ruminating about the whys and wherefores of societal maladies. The book is a good read, for the entertainment, of course, and for the social commentary as well. Highly recommended. - Charles Whipple, Japan; author and editor

A particular difficulty with short stories is that they are exactly that – short. All too often they can be over before they have really begun, leaving the reader somewhat frustrated. But Nik Morton has managed to create a collection of individual stories in this particular book which are absolute little gems. The pace of each is perfectly judged to reach its conclusion at just the right time and in just the right way. Nik has also managed in many of them to weave in topical Spanish themes and issues such as immigrants trying to get into Spain from North Africa, drug running, memories of the Civil War and the corruption of Land Grab in Valencia to name but a few. I can thoroughly recommend this book. Not only will the tales appeal to general lovers of short stories but in particular those with experience of living in Spain will I'm sure feel a certain resonance with these stories. - Amazon reviewer, June 2014

Stories to keep you wanting more ... and more. Tales of reminiscence by a sleuth in sunny Spain which ensure you keep your eyes open until you've reached the end of one in time to let your head fall on the pillow - until morning. Thankyou Nik, for making my nights unbroken and worth waiting for. – Jane Bwye, author of *Breath of Africa* and *Grass Shoots*

… a marvelous collection of short stories linked by a common protagonist, the private investigator Leon Cazador. Yet, each story is unique in setting and plot, drawing on the author's remarkable breadth of knowledge and extraordinarily full life, spiced by a genuine loathing for evil and wrong-doing. We learn a great deal

Leon Cazador, P.I.

about the history, culture, lore, and landscape of Spain and meet a diverse cast of characters, as Cazador sees to it that a variety of miscreants, petty and grand, are appropriately done in. Mr. Morton is a gifted writer, a modern-day Aesop, only more complex, providing entertaining stories, each with a moral. You have no idea of the treat that is in store for you. – Charles Ameringer, author of *The Old Spook.*

Nik Morton

Other books by Nik Morton

Bullets for a Ballot
Coffin for Cash
Death for a Dove
Continuity Girl (also featuring We Fell Below the Earth)
An Evil Trade
The Bread of Tears
Chill of the Shadow
Gifts from a Dead Race – Collected stories vol.1
Nourish a Blind Life – Collected stories vol.2
Visitors – Collected stories vol.3
Codename Gaby – Collected stories vol.4
I Celebrate Myself – Collected stories vol.5
A Fistful of Legends (Anthology Editor)

The Tana Standish psychic spy series:
Mission: Prague (#1)
Mission: Tehran (#2)
Mission: Khyber (#3)

The Avenging Cat series:
Catalyst (#1)
Catacomb (#2)
Cataclysm (#3)

Non-fiction
Write a Western in 30 Days – with plenty of bullet points!
Old Shoes and Medals (memoir)

Westerns writing as Ross Morton:
The Magnificent Mendozas
The $300 Man
Old Guns
Blind Justice at Wedlock
Last Chance Saloon
Death at Bethesda Falls

Fantasy writing as Morton Faulkner
Floreskand: Wings
Floreskand: King

Leon Cazador, P.I.

Dedication

To Jennifer, with love, as usual. And of course, to Hannah, Harry, Darius and Suri.

And to Margaret and Neil as a reminder of your times in Spain.

And lastly, to my long-lost brother, Paul Leon Andrews Sutton, his wife Michelle and daughter Amelia.

Acknowledgements

Thanks to Paul Kavanagh and Rosemary Samuel for first spotting and buying into Leon Cazador.

Thanks also to Jake Lowe, Sandra Shankland and David Cranmer for publishing his stories, too.

To Charles T. Whipple, fellow editor, writer and friend, for your insight at the other end of the world!

Thanks also to Stephanie Patterson, Christine McPherson and Laurence Patterson.

Leon Cazador, P.I.

Contents

Introduction - 13

Processionary Penitents - 17
Relic Hunters - 29
Night Fishing - 41
Adopted Country - 47
Grave Concerns - 53
Fair Cop - 59
Bitter Almonds - 65
Shattered Dream - 71
Off Plan - 75
Dragon Lady - 81
Cry Wolf - 89
Endangered Species - 95
Big Noise - 103
Pueblo Pride - 113
Duty Bound - 121
Tragic Roundabout - 129
Burning Issue - 135
Lonely Hearts - 141
Prickly Pair - 147
Criminal Damage - 153
Pigeon-Hearted - 159
Inn Time - 169
Gone Missing – 177

Glossary - 189
Afterword – 191

Printing History

The individual stories in this collection were published in the following periodicals:

Shattered Dream © 2005 published in *The Coastal Press*, November
Bitter Almonds © 2005 published in *The Coastal Press*, December
Off Plan © 2006 published in *The Coastal Press*, January
Adopted Country © 2006 published in *The Coastal Press*, February
Cry Wolf © 2006 published in *The Coastal Press*, March
Dragon Lady © 2006 published in *The Coastal Press*, April
Pueblo Pride © 2006 shorter variation published in *Torrevieja Another Look Anthology*, May
Endangered Species © 2006 published in *The Coastal Press*, June
Fair Cop © 2006 published in *The Coastal Press*, July
Night Fishing © 2006 published in *The Coastal Press*, September
Lonely Hearts © 2006 published in *The Coastal Press*, November
Burning Issue © 2007 published in *The Coastal Press*, January
Relic Hunters © 2007 published in *The Coastal Press*, July
Grave Concerns © 2007 published in *The Coastal Press*, October
Duty Bound © 2007 published in *The Coastal Press*, November
Criminal Damage © 2008 published in *The Levante Journal*, January
Tragic Roundabout © 2008 published in *The Coastal Press*, March
Prickly Pair © 2008 published in *The Coastal Press,* April
Big Noise highly commended by *Writers Forum*, September 2006, Top Ten "Justice" competition of Mace & Jones: © 2008 published in *The Levante Journal*, December
Pigeon-Hearted © 2009 published in *The New Coastal Press*, November
Inn Time © 2009 published in *Costa TV Times,* December
Gone Missing © 2011 published by Beat to a Pulp, November
Processionary Penitents © 2014 published in *Crooked Cats' Tales Anthology*

Leon Cazador, P.I.

INTRODUCTION

A few years ago, I received a telephone call from a Spanish private investigator, Leon Cazador. He'd heard of my efforts with a novel about a nun who used to be a cop (*The Bread of Tears*), and wanted me to write up some of his cases in a similar vein in first person narrative.

I've lost count of the number of approaches I've had from people wanting me to ghost write their autobiographies; it's gratifying but any such venture entails many months of intense work and distracts me from other planned projects. I was inclined to turn down Señor Cazador until he said, "I thought you captured the voice of Sister Rose perfectly. I feel you could do it for me, too." Suitably flattered, I arranged a meeting.

Over *café cortado*, I found that he was a fascinating raconteur and more importantly, he had a good story—or rather stories—to tell. As a result, I began writing Leon Cazador short stories, purportedly as fiction, all of which seem to have been well received.

The world needs brave souls like Leon Cazador who is not afraid to bring the ungodly to justice and so help, in his own words, *to hold back the encroaching night of unreason.*

"My allegiance is split because I'm half-English and half-Spanish," he says. "Mother had a whirlwind romance with a Spanish waiter but happily it didn't end when the holiday was over. The waiter pursued her to England and they were married."

Leon was born in Spain and has a married sister, Pilar, and an older brother, Juan, who is an officer in the *Guardia Civil*. Leon Cazador sometimes operates in disguise under several aliases, among them Carlos Ortiz Santos, his little tribute to the fabled fictional character, Simon Templar.

As a consequence of dealing with the authorities and criminals, Leon has observed in his two home countries the gradual deterioration of effective law enforcement and the disintegration of respect. "My name translated into English is 'Lion Hunter'," he says. "The Spanish sounds less pretentious, I think."

At our first meeting, he said, "When I was growing up in England, I never imagined there would be no-go areas in those great cities, places where the shadow of light falls on streets and minds." I thought he was bordering on the poetic then: the shadow of light is darkness, after all.

Now that he has returned to live in Spain, he finds that it is not so bad here, though he admits that he has seen many changes over the last thirty-odd years, most of them good, yet some to be deplored. "It is heartening to see that family cohesion is still strong in most areas, but even that age-old stability is under threat. Yet, some *urbanizaciones* more resemble towns on the frontier of the Old West, where mayors can be bought, where lawlessness is endemic and civilised behaviour seems to have barely a foothold. Even so, most nights you can walk the streets and feel safe here in Spain."

Leon has led an interesting life. As Spain's conscription didn't cease until 2001, he decided to jump rather than be pushed and joined the Army, graduating as an Artillery Lieutenant. About a year later, he joined the Spanish Foreign Legion's Special Operations Company (*Bandera de operaciones especiales de la legión*) and was trained in the United States at Fort Bragg, where he built up his considerable knowledge about clandestine activities and weapons. Some months afterwards, he was recruited into the CESID (*Centro Superior de Informacion de la Defensa*), which later became the CNI (*Centro Nacional de Inteligencia*). Unlike most Western democracies, Spain runs a single intelligence organisation to handle both domestic and foreign risks.

He is one of those fortunate individuals capable of learning a foreign language with ease: he grew up bilingual, speaking English and Spanish, and soon learned Portuguese, French, German, Arabic, Chinese, and basic Japanese. Part of his intelligence gathering entailed his transfer to the Spanish Embassy in Washington, D.C. There, he met several useful contacts in the intelligence community, and at the close of the Soviet occupation of Afghanistan he embarked on a number of secret missions to that blighted land with CIA operatives. By the time the Soviet withdrawal was a reality, Leon was transferred to the Spanish

Leon Cazador, P.I.

Embassy in Tokyo, where he liaised with both intelligence and police organisations. Secret work followed in China, the Gulf and Yugoslavia.

In 1987, Leon was attached to a secret section of MI6 to assist operatives in Colombia.

Although he has been decorated four times in theatres of conflict, reports suggest his bravery justifies at least three more medals.

A year after witnessing the atrocity of the Twin Towers while stationed with the United Nations, he returned to civilian life and set up a private investigation firm.

During periods of leave and while stationed in Spain, he established a useful network of contacts in law enforcement, notably the *Guardia Civil*. One of his early cases resulted in him becoming financially set for life, so now he conducts his crusade against villains of all shades, and in the process attempts to save the unwary from the clutches of conmen, rogues and crooks.

These then are some of Leon Cazador's cases, in his own words.

Nik Morton
Alicante, Spain

Leon Cazador, P.I.

PROCESSIONARY PENITENTS

"Oh, my God!" Sebastian Okoro exclaimed. "They're Ku Klux Klan!" Even in the lamp-lit street, I felt sure his ebony complexion had paled. His eyes started, whites showing in the flickering flames from the torches. He was serious. This was unlike him, a dedicated agent of the National Crime Agency. I decided to disabuse my friend of the KKK idea fast.

"Seb, don't worry, this is quite normal." I gestured at the colourful slowly passing procession. "It's a religious ceremony that goes back to the Middle-Ages and has nothing to do with racial prejudice!"

"You're sure?"

"Yes, of course. It's Spain's Holy Week – *Semana Santa*. Similar processions are happening all over the country."

He visibly relaxed. "All right... What are we doing here, watching a procession? I thought you were going to finger Franco Roldan for me." Seb was a workaholic, so I wasn't surprised at his tone.

I pointed to the phalanx of men carrying candles, striding in front of the enormous religious float that depicted the Passion of Christ; they wore silk robes or nazarenos and pointed hoods, capirotes, with eye-holes. "The men in the conical hoods represent penitents from the old days."

"So?"

"So, it just happens that two of them are due to exhibit penitence, though they don't know it yet. And one of them is Roldan..."

He sighed. "Must you always talk in riddles, Leon?"

I grinned. "No, not always. Enjoy the procession."

This particular float was over a hundred years old. The Brotherhood who owned it belonged to "The Beautiful Virgin", a fraternity that had been in existence since the late 1500s.

A brass band performed its own processional march.

Despite their similar garb, each individual penitent under the disguise was unique, in subtle ways. Their shoes differed, and their robes didn't always drape their full length; a good number of the bottoms of the men's trousers showed – brown, blue, grey and black. Breadth of shoulders varied too. I pointed to a short man wearing brown deck shoes and fawn trousers. "Pablo Saura, an architect..." I pointed again. "And there's Roldan." Roldan was a head taller than the architect.

"He looks pretty pious," Seb seethed, "carrying that wooden cross! Hypocrite!"

I nodded. "He reminds me of Mafia men I've met, who have no qualms about going to confession in the morning and slaughtering some poor soul in the evening."

"They don't have a conscience, Leon."

"Perhaps not. But the law will catch up with them, eventually."

Seb grinned. "Are we calling in the police now, then?"

I shook my head. "If you wish. It's your case. They're happy to let you direct the action against Roldan." True enough. As soon as he arrived, Sebastian had been in touch with both the National Police and the Guardia Civil in the area. It wasn't only a matter of courtesy. It was now standard international policing procedure, the only way to successfully combat international crime. Resources and data were pooled to better effect an arrest.

Roldan fled England when his counterfeiting ring was busted by another friend of mine, Detective Inspector Alan Pointer. I'd worked with Alan and his sergeant Carol Bassett some years back, when the NCA was called SOCA. They were a good team: "let slip the dogs of law!" was a phrase attached to them. Since then, however, Alan had become a reclusive agent, tending to work only at night.

There'd been ructions when it was learned Roldan skipped the country dressed in a niqab and using a false passport; this was almost a repetition of the escape of police killer Mustafa Jama in 2006. The Border Agency was red-faced - again. No heads rolled, though. If somebody uses an "inappropriate word" with regard to race or gender, he'll be hounded out of his career; but if a civil servant is proved incompetent and criminally negligent, he might get a slapped wrist. The brave new world of law enforcement in Britain – political correctness is more important than catching and punishing criminals; and that particular contagion was spreading to all European law agencies. And Seb wondered why I'd decided to get out and go it alone as a private eye!

I preferred it this way: no red tape, no accountability. The system worked and helped snare the ungodly.

Seb bit his lip. "Why delay?"

"You said his organization in Brighton needed input from elsewhere, didn't you?"

"Yes. Every indication showed he was a major operator, but not the source."

"Exactly. I think he will contact his source here and try to set up another counterfeiting shop." It wasn't money they copied; that was getting harder, particularly with the newly released euro notes; no, they duplicated movies on DVD. The market was already flooded with bad copies, many from Chinese outlets; the local police in most coastal towns regularly raided warehouses, confiscated the counterfeit products, mostly watches, handbags, CDs and DVDs, and then employed steam rollers to crush the contraband. But Roldan's copies were so good they could pass off as originals. Apologists for the illegal copiers said that if the new movies were sold at sensible prices, the trade in copies would virtually dry up. That's not how commerce works, though; anything new gets a high starting price, anticipating a surge in demand from the instant gratification generation.

"So," Seb asked, "what has the architect got to do with anything?"

***

Pablo Saura came from an extensive family, many of whom found themselves in positions of authority and, naturally, Pablo won the architect tenders for work in small towns up and down eastern Spain. Nepotism is endemic in Spain, and always has been. Thanks to his familial connections, his star was in the ascendant. Unfortunately, as his success grew, the quality of his work declined. Hubris.

"Tomorrow morning," I said, "I'll pay him a visit."

"Should I come along?"

"No, Seb. You don't want to get involved."

He looked askance at me. He knew a little about my methods; they were not always quite within the law. Then he shrugged. "What about Roldan?"

"Plans are taking shape. I'll let you know."

"There you go again – going all mysterious on me!"

I laughed. "Must be my secret service training," I whispered.

***

It was quiet as I walked along the village street; most of the two-storey buildings were old, in need of fresh plaster or paint. A cock crowed from an inner courtyard. It wasn't early, gone nine. At the end of the road a white van was parked with rear doors open, its interior displaying wooden trays crammed with bread, empanadas, and ensaimadas. Attired in his white apron, the baker stood on the pavement, filling a wicker basket with loaves. Above, an elderly woman in black leaned over her balcony rail – Señora Barrantes – and called down to him; then she hauled on the rope, tugging the basket up. I passed the baker, exchanged *buenos días* and turned right, round the corner.

Across the road, on the left and between two older dwellings, a ruined house stood, windows gaping like empty eyes, its upper storey caved-in. Directly opposite the now derelict building, I stopped and turned, knocked on the facing door. It opened and a bead curtain was swept aside by thin arthritic fingers. "Sí?" an ancient man croaked.

"Señor Quinto, I'm Leon Cazador. I've spoken to your wife."

"Yes, yes, come in." He stood aside to allow me to pass into the hallway, then slammed the door shut. The beads rattled as they settled behind us. He led me along the passage, past two doors, then turned left into a quite large kitchen, its floor covered in russet-coloured tiles. In the middle of the room stood a rough-hewn wooden table, and four matching chairs. An Iberian ham hung from a hook in the ceiling, over the sink, where an old woman stood, hunched back to me. She turned, the side of her face partially sunken, the bone structure crushed.

Madalena Quinto had been visiting her neighbour, Bonita Ruiz, in the house opposite when the earthquake struck on the afternoon of 11 May 2011. Her friend, Bonita, was buried under the rubble; Madalena survived with a shattered shoulder and face.

In all, nine died and dozens were injured. It was the worst quake the region had experienced since the 1950s, measuring 5.1 magnitude. The experts labelled it "moderate", though those affected saw it differently. Ancient structures were seriously damaged, including the historical Espolón Tower of Lorca Castle, the Hermitage of San Clemente and the Convent of Virgen de Las Huertas. As this occurred two months to the very day after the devastating Japanese earthquake and tsunami, it was understandable that fears over further cataclysmic events increased the potential for panic.

The wheels of the law, the courts and the village administration grind slowly. Madalena Quinto accused architect Pablo Saura of negligence when designing the second storey extension of her friend Bonita's house. It's a common sight, single storey homes being extended upwards. Naturally, planning permission and inspections should be the norm; that's in the ideal world. Kickbacks to town planners and officials sometimes skirt these safety essentials. Perhaps if an earthquake had not occurred, then the new second storey might not have collapsed? Two other extensions in the village, designed by Saura, had suffered from serious structural defects and cracks.

The upshot of it was that Saura was due to appear in court in two months' time. Saura's argument was that his design was sound; the blame lay with the builders. The plans were impounded, pending the case.

She moved away from the sink and settled in a chair. I sat opposite, elbows on the table.

"He will wriggle free," she wheezed. The bones of her chest had suffered trauma too.

"He will become a penitent, have no fear, Dona Quinto," I assured her.

Time for the architect to meet Carlos Ortiz Santos.

***

He answered on the second ring. "Saura."

"Señor, you don't know me, but I have a friend in the judiciary who might help you in your present difficulty. The word is that your architect's plans will go against you…"

"Who is this?"

"I am called Carlos Santos, and..."

"You're right, I don't know you." His tone and the pause that followed hinted that he was about to hang up.

"The plans," I said rapidly, "they can be altered to help your case, señor..."

Silence. But he must have heard; the connection hadn't clicked off.

"What are you implying, Señor Santos?"

"Perhaps we could meet to discuss the subject further. I can recommend a quiet place, where we wouldn't be disturbed."

"I would rather..."

"Señor, this is a delicate matter. I wish to preserve my anonymity. I have a safe house... it is not far from your office, as it happens..."

I heard paper being shifted. "I won't be free until 4p.m."

"That is fine." I told him the address.

"I know it. As you say, not far."

"Bring five thousand euros – the first half, to show good faith."

"Five thou... And that's just half ... Ten altogether?"

"Your career, it is worth more than that, surely?"

"Why, yes, of course it is, but..."

"Remember, Señor Saura, the case against you is liable to ruin your career, should it prevail..."

"Yes... I will be there..."

I hung up. First phase complete: architect drawn in.

***

"I hope I don't need to draw you a picture, Señor Saura?" I adjusted the tinted spectacles on my nose, shifted in the leather armchair, leaned forward and stroked my false moustache. "You want me to arrange the substitution of a more favourable copy of your building plans, correct...?"

His small close-set eyes glared. "Of course I do!" He was thin, impeccably dressed in a charcoal grey suit, sitting on the edge of the sofa. "That's why I'm here!" We were alone in the lounge of a safe house I'd used before. Spartan furnishing – a lounge diner with two armchairs, the sofa, a small dining table and four chairs, a sideboard and wall sconces for most necessary additional lighting.

There were two small bedrooms and a bathroom. "That's why I've brought the money – all five thousand euros!"

"Well…" I waved an arm, shrugged dismissively, as if I didn't really care about money, but felt that it was expected in this kind of transaction. "A consideration, no?"

Saura closed his eyes; his eyeballs moved under the lids, as if he was calculating the money, a euro at a time. He ran a hand over his face, opened his eyes. "Very well." He ground his teeth together. I wondered if he would rather grind down those who opposed him and his schemes; grind them into the earth.

"You should have been more thorough with your plans, señor. Then this unsavoury transaction would not prove necessary."

"More thorough? Why? We're talking about townsfolk, little people. Their silly schemes are a piffling trifle to me!"

"But you took on the work, no?"

"I regard it as pin money. I can draw up the appropriate plans in an hour or so – and charge them for two days' work!" He slapped the chair arm. "Now, important work for the council, that takes precedence every time!" He chuckled. "For that, I might make the effort to check my figures, confirm the stress points and so on! But for the little people, they don't pay me enough to do that. Not nearly enough! They should not have raised that *denuncia* against me. I am a professional!"

"Of course. I quite understand." I felt like grinding my fist in his face then. He exhibited a certain arrogance that I'd witnessed in a number of so-called professional men.

He pulled out a silk handkerchief, wiped his brow. "So, Señor Santos, when can you arrange for the switch?"

"Tomorrow."

"That fast?"

"I thought it best for our man to act promptly for you..." I held out my hand.

He removed a brown paper envelope from his breast pocket, passed it over. Such envelopes had become a cliché, yet were still used.

I opened it and scrutinized the contents, counted the notes.

He growled, "It's all there!"

"I don't doubt it." I continued to count it, marking aloud each thousand, ensuring that my actions were in plain view of the concealed camera.

With his own words, he was the architect of his fall from grace.

***

Next day, Saura was found entirely cocooned in architect's plans, all fastened tightly with adhesive tape. In his chrysalis, his feet in a wicker basket, he dangled above the pavement, the rope secured round his waist and attached to a pulley on the balcony above.

He resembled a giant nest of processionary caterpillars. Their white lacy cocoons cling to fir trees any time from January through to April, depending on the weather. To begin with they're moths' eggs; when they hatch, the larvae feast on the pine needles then, as caterpillars, crawl down the tree to the ground, marching in single file, nose to tail, in search of somewhere to dig underground and pupate, until the end of the summer, when they emerge as moths. Their very fine hairs are particularly nasty, causing rashes, itches or serious inflammation and allergic reactions. Unwary dogs have choked with swollen throats. As hairy caterpillars, they seem immune to prey; as pupae, they're lunch for the Hoopoe; and as moths they're feasted on by bats. I wasn't sure which stage Saura was in, dangling there, but I anticipated that he'd be devoured by the press and the courts.

Señora Barrantes, the elderly lady in black, leaned over her balcony and laughed, clapping her hands at the sight. The two Guardia Civil officers in attendance were not so amused. Pinned to the architect's chest was a note, which stated that Saura had paid a bribe for someone to steal the building plans from the courthouse; it also advised that a copy of the secretly filmed meeting was with the press.

Later that day, the word spread, the video going viral. The newspaper *Información* broke the story, complete with a link to the video of the bribe. This wasn't the first time the newspaper had promulgated a sting operation and, judging by the corruption still prevalent, I didn't think it would be the last.

Kidnapping is against the law; there are no mitigating circumstances. However, I feel that where law-breakers are concerned, since they don't respect the law, they don't always deserve its protection. Once I'd seen Saura to the door, out of view from the camera, I applied a strangle-hold, his windpipe in the crook of my elbow; it only took eight seconds to render him unconscious; I was careful not to exceed that time as death could result. I prefer this for the less dangerous ungodly; the dangerous ones, I have no qualms about hitting or squeezing the carotid artery – again, with care, as this too can be fatal.

When he was suitably wrapped for delivery, I bundled him in his car.

Despite his small stature, it hadn't been easy to suspend him there in the early hours, after the festival lovers had finally retired. First, I had to clamber on to the roof of his vehicle to reach the dangling rope, and then I heaved him up and made sure he was safely secured. Only then could I drive off. I'd worn gloves throughout this phase. I abandoned the car outside his villa.

***

I knocked on the Quinto door and it opened almost immediately. "Come in, come in, Señor Cazador!" The old man hastened me into the lounge, pointed to the television screen. I was in time to see Saura shouting that he was "a professional"

"He is finished! My wife will have satisfaction!"

I fished out the five thousand euros. "You can probably make use of this, too. Small compensation for the distress that man has put you through."

His eyes watered. Pride vied with common sense as his hands wavered, and then he took the money. "Gracías, Señor Cazador."

I nodded at the TV screen. "I don't think Saura is ever going to make it in Hollywood." I pointed to the rack of a dozen or so DVDs on the sideboard. "Stick to legal movies, with happy endings like this one."

***

"Mr Santos, it's good of you to make it," said Franco Roldan, opening his villa's front door. He was dressed like a movie star, multi-coloured short-sleeved shirt, white slacks, tan pumps. His hair was thick, curly and dyed auburn. He held out a hand.

We shook and he ushered me inside, and said to the goon at the door, "Back to your post, Rico!" Rico was one of two armed men; three bikini-clad women lounged by the swimming pool, sipping cocktails, but didn't seem fazed by the sight of the sentries with their Star Z-84 sub-machine guns slung over their shoulders.

Roldan led me along a tiled passage, the walls adorned with modern art, though I use the "art" word loosely. Art is a matter of taste – and Roldan's was all bad.

"I'm not the last to arrive, am I?" I queried, allowing a little anxiety in my tone.

"No, no, we have Nico still to come. Then we can haggle about distribution, no?"

"I'm not particularly good at haggling," I said.

"No matter. I will ensure that all of my associates do well out of this business." We entered and he gestured at a table where five men and a woman sat. A couple looked Eastern European, the rest Latin. I knew three from Ministry of Interior mug-shots. I detected a little tension as introductions were made.

I sat at the table, laid my Samsung Galaxy mobile phone in front of me.

"Are you expecting a call?" Roldan asked.

"No. But it serves as my burglar alarm."

Roldan turned to the others. "His burglar alarm!" He laughed. "He is worried about being burgled!"

A couple of the men laughed too; the others either didn't seem amused.

Nico arrived and I noticed that the tension in the room eased.

"Right, let's get down to business," Roldan said. "My factory is producing two thousand DVD copies a day. A-list movies, acquired from good sources." He opened his laptop, clicked a couple of keys, and swung it round to show us the screen.

He was right; this was the latest film, just released in the US; good quality. I suspected that those gathered here wouldn't like the ending, though…

"Where is your factory?" Nico asked.

"Crevillente."

"A carpet warehouse?"

"Seems like a good cover," I observed.

At least Roldan got the joke, smiling thinly. "Quite." He then reeled off his outlets, his couriers and the days when stocks would be replenished. He was a good organizer, and very thorough.

After we'd agreed our roles, I asked, "Can you guarantee your source of films?"

Leon Cazador, P.I.

Roldan nodded. "Emil is very reliable. He has a number of insiders he can call upon."

"Good." That was all I required. According to Seb, suspicions had rested upon a guy named Emil Chapman in California. This was the proof they needed. Idly, I switched off my phone's voice recorder app, and then fingered the auto-dial.

***

Two shots were fired outside. Roldan stood and exclaimed, "What the hell...?"

I retrieved from my ankle holster the lightweight Colt Officer's ACP LW automatic and levelled it at all eight of them. "You can try to rush me – the magazine only holds six cartridges."

Nobody moved.

"Very sensible."

Seconds later, Seb entered alongside a Civil Guard Lieutenant.

"You seem to have everything under control," Seb said.

I nodded. "The details you want are on my phone."

The Guardia Civil, the National Police and the local police had raided the villa en masse, Seb accompanying them. The women in bikinis scampered out of the way as armed lawmen scaled the walls, wounded the two sentries, skirted the swimming pool and burst into the lounge. They found me with the guilty parties. The entire operation was filmed by the Guardia Civil.

Roldan and his cronies were read their rights and handcuffed. "Your days are numbered, Santos!" Roldan grated.

"At least they won't be under lock and key," I said. This wasn't the first death threat I'd received in my disguise; I felt sure it wouldn't be the last.

The haul from the subsequent search was considerable: eight hand-guns, two machine pistols, four kilos of cocaine, a hundred illegal DVDs, four laptops, €40,000 and two stolen cars. As well as the incriminating information about the illegal outlets and sources both here in Spain and in California.

Under heavy armed guard, Roldan and his cronies were led out of the villa, in single file procession, and loaded into the back of two Civil Guard Mercedes Sprinter wagons.

I eyed Seb. "That'll be the last procession he'll be in for some time."

Nik Morton

Leon Cazador, P.I.

RELIC HUNTERS

Angel Ramos held his breath as he carefully unlatched then lifted the ornate lid off the rosewood box. A distinctive smell emerged like a palpable thing, together with a fine miasma of dust that floated in the sunbeams slanting through the hotel window. It was the aroma of old parchment or vellum that harboured the dust of centuries.

"This is only the second time in almost seven hundred years that this chest has been opened," he said in a hushed voice.

"You sound like you've found the Holy Grail," I said, watching his latex-gloved fingers gently lift out a vellum scroll, one of several.

Delicately, he used a small brush to clear away the fine film of dust. "Your jest might be close to the truth, Leon."

This surprised me. Angel was not prone to exaggerate. I'd known him since 1987 when we met in Afghanistan, of all places. He was on an archaeological dig, specially sanctioned by Gorbachev himself, and I was disguised as a sheepherder to spy on the Russian invaders. Strange how the world has turned since.

A fit septuagenarian, his straggly hair was white with streaks of gray. Angel's shoulders were stooped, probably from studying too many buried relics. Behind his spectacles, his dark brown eyes still held a glint of youthful excitement.

Holding his breath again, he unrolled the vellum and scanned the contents, his thin lips pursed. He seemed mesmerised, yet his eyes kept moving, reading. The hotel room dimmed into obscurity around us. Only this ancient letter appeared real.

Finally, he lowered the letter to the table and let out his breath. "This is very good," he said, and somehow I knew that it was an understatement.

I leaned closer. The writing was Latin. At the foot of the page was a wax seal, its patina tarnished.

"It's written by Ruy Menéndez, a Knight Templar."

"Really? What does he say?"

Angel said, "I'll paraphrase for you. They hid their treasure to prevent it from getting into the grasping hands of the king and the Pope."

"Yes, I've read about the period. Plenty of scope for myth, I always thought."

"Quite so. And he gives instructions on how to find the treasure."

"Incredible!" I replied, not knowing what else to say.

"*Sí*, a voice from the past," Angel said and sneezed. "The dust, it is an occupational hazard."

***

The dust of the past swirled and dislodged samples of history from my memory. In 1307 Philip IV ordered the arrest of every Templar in France and commandeered all their land and property. He made false claims to justify his actions, and the power-and-money-grasping French Pope Clement V backed up Philip. But they didn't get all their own way, it seems, since a church council voted against this suppression of the Templars and indeed they found the Templars outside France innocent of the charges.

Like some petulant modern day politician or EU official, Clement ignored their findings and the Templars were hunted down like dogs throughout Europe. Their property was either confiscated or transferred to another military order, the Hospitalers.

All of the captured knights had to confess to crimes they had not committed or face being burned at the stake.

This was the uncompromising stuff of history. And now a piece of that history was here in the agricultural town of Bullas, in this two star hotel room.

Dangerous times, then. I repressed a shudder, fancifully imagining one of the persecuted Templars looking over our shoulders.

Dangerous times now as well. Because Angel was being hounded by a rival archaeologist, Lucas Moffat, who was seeking the same treasure. I knew Moffat; he was both ruthless and unforgiving.

These days I rarely worked as a bodyguard. Age affected my reflexes, made them less sharp. Besides, I was reluctant to take a bullet for any employer. Old friends happened to be different, so

I'd decided to carry my Astra A-100 in its shoulder holster under my tan suit jacket.

"Do you want to find the treasure now?" I asked. If it was my treasure, I'd be halfway there already, I thought.

"No, we'll set out first thing tomorrow," he said, showing great willpower. "Tonight, I think, we should open a bottle of Cava."

I allowed myself one glass and Angel finished the bottle and went to bed.

***

Angel had been working on an undemanding dig in rocky northwest Murcia, hoping to uncover Roman artifacts. The land was barren save for gorse and rampant aloe. He remembered hearing the distinctive call of a number of stonechats, like pebbles being rubbed together, and then, eerily, they fell silent. A few seconds later, the earthquake happened. The area had tremors between two and five on the Richter scale. At the time, he didn't know what the measurement was, only that he was thrust off his feet and rolled down a rocky slope, landing against a large boulder. The second or two that the tremor lasted seemed much longer, he said afterwards. His entire body shook, even when the land stilled. When he sat up, he was surprised to find a rocky cleft had opened up into a wide fissure. Something glinted in the gap, about ten feet below.

Probably the sun reflecting on slate or white stone of some sort, he thought, but his curiosity was aroused. Forgetful about his creaking bones, Angel rummaged in his pack and grabbed a torch. He clambered into the newly made fissure and found enough firm footholds to descend slowly and confidently. He let out a gasp of surprise when he reached the glinting object. It was a Roman belt buckle.

He climbed further down, about another twenty feet. The odd falling pebble made an echoing sound. He fancied he heard the resumption of the stonechats above, which was reassuring, suggesting that there were no aftershocks imminent. Very tentatively indeed, Angel lowered his light frame into a large underground room with a tiled floor, complete with remarkably preserved ancient bulky furniture. His torch revealed a set of seven pewter goblets on a sideboard. In their centre was a gold cross, very similar to that found at nearby Caravaca. And on another table was the rosewood chest.

Two doors led out of the room, but over the centuries, they'd been blocked by falling rock, and the lintels had skewed. He ran the torch beam over each in turn but could not detect any booby traps.

Angel found it hard to recount the feelings that swamped him at that moment of discovery.

The carved design on the chest signified that it once belonged to the Knights Templar.

Angel thrust the chest inside his shirt, buttoned it up and climbed back out through the fissure.

Before leaving the site, he made sure there was no evidence that he'd been there, brushing away footprints. He scanned the surrounding area and was certain he could find the place again.

Almost in a dream, he retraced his steps to his car. Sitting in front of the steering wheel, he eased the chest out from his shirt and gently put it on the passenger seat. It was so precious, he wanted to fit the seatbelt across it, but shrugged the silly idea aside. Just drive carefully, he told himself.

Once in his Murcia apartment, he poured a glass of brandy with trembling hands and then opened the chest with stringent care.

The phone call disturbed him as soon as he lifted the lid, spoiling his mood.

"I'm curious about that box, dear Angel," said the soft rather soporific voice.

Moffat! It was pointless asking how the damnable man knew. Moffat had plenty of contacts. He was greedy and without scruple. Angel had probably been watched as he left his car and entered his apartment block.

"Curiosity killed the cat," he replied and lowered the receiver. His choice of words seemed rather chilling, he realised as an afterthought.

He was still trembling when I arrived at his apartment door in response to his urgent summons.

***

For centuries, caves had been searched for the hidden Templar riches in this mountain range. Rumours abounded that one of the owners of the troglodyte houses had found the treasure long ago.

Others suggested that it had been found when Franco's grandiose dam project at Cenajo neared completion.

Now, it seemed, we would find out.

"It depends, Angel."

He nodded as I drove up the winding mountain road. "I know, friend. The landscape has changed in seven hundred years!"

"At least they didn't hide it on the coast!"

Angel laughed. "That would have made some builder very happy, no?"

We drove on in silence. Two hundred yards along a goat track. It seemed perfectly feasible that some of these old trails had been in existence for hundreds, if not thousands, of years. There was a particular outcrop of rock that the parchment had described. At the right angle, it resembled the draped bowed face of the Virgin. Here, I parked the four-by-four and got out. I looped the coil of climbing rope over my head then put on my Norfolk hat and clutched a rucksack containing bottled water and tools.

"Ready?" I asked.

"Yes, old friend," Angel said. "But don't rush; if it's there it can wait a little longer to be discovered."

"True enough," I said and led the way up the rock-strewn slope.

Behind us were abandoned terraces that had once been tilled and harvested. Above, the rugged land was only capable of sustaining prickly pears, shrubs and aloes.

After a while, I slowed my pace as I realised that Angel was finding it difficult terrain to negotiate.

A gully beckoned and at its end, a few ramshackle ruins were dotted about. The dwellings were probably abandoned when the stream ceased to flow. One of many aborted villages. On the other hand, it could have been depleted by the depredations of the Civil War and its bloodthirsty aftermath.

"Hard to believe people lived here," Angel panted.

I pointed. "There's the washing trough." Once a gathering place for the village women, only red soil and stones now choked the receptacles where water had splashed to the sound of gossip and laughter.

We both paced out twenty steps to the right of the old trough and moved round a bend in the slightly rising track. Above, to our left, was a crumbling watchtower, a distinct marker.

"The windmill," Angel wheezed, gesturing above and to our right. This was dilapidated, its walls a warm dun colour against the stark blue sky. Its wooden sails had long ago disintegrated into dust.

"So far so good," I said. In the back of my mind, I wondered how many earthquakes had riven this land over the centuries. It would be surprising to find every landmark intact and visible.

Slowly, we climbed up to the ancient windmill.

Inside, rubble and dust cluttered the floor. Stones jutted out where stairs had once led to the upper level. There was no machinery and no roof, and the sky was clear, the sun beating down on us. A lizard darted to our left and vanished in a shadowy crack in the wall.

Eight paces from the door marked the spot. I scraped my boot toe across the floor to make a rough X. Then I unfastened the small shovel from my pack and moved the rubble away. After five minutes, I removed my Norfolk and wiped my forehead with my sleeve. It took me about fifteen minutes to dig and scrape away the surface soil and stones. I stood back, straightening my body and whispered, "What do you make of that?"

"Oh my God, Leon," breathed Angel.

Quite a hushed response, considering I'd uncovered a stone trapdoor and its rusted metal ring.

My mouth was dry but it had nothing to do with the heat or thirst. I felt sure that Angel was on the brink of some great discovery.

Without speaking, we both knelt down and our knives scraped away an age of dust from around the oblong shape of the trapdoor and its ring handle.

Finally, I asked Angel to step back, and I leant forward. I wrapped my fingers round the metal ring and got a purchase. Knees bent, back straight, I heaved.

The trapdoor creaked and so did my muscles.

It grated and lifted very slowly. Rubble fell into the dark square opening; it took a few seconds to land. "It's a long way down," I said.

Angel switched on a torch while I lowered the stone trapdoor to the floor.

He leaned with one hand against the wall, the other on his heaving chest. "I don't think I can do this, Leon."

"Are you all right?"

He nodded, seemingly unable to speak.

"Shall we close it and tell the authorities? You'll still get half."

He grinned. "Like hell we will!" He gestured at the dark entrance. "Might I ask you to go for me?"

While I was honoured, I shook my head. "This is your moment, Angel. It must be you."

"Thank you, old friend." He clasped a hand on my shoulder and wheezed. "But some things are not worth dying for, not even fantastic treasures!"

"That's a matter of opinion!" barked Lucas Moffat, standing in the doorway. One eye was covered with a leather patch, the other glinted. His lips broadened into a smile. "This is Torres, by the way." Behind him was a thickset bearded man holding a Llama Comanche revolver, its snout aimed at Angel and me.

***

Torres wasn't comfortable following me down the rope into the darkness. He should have known that as long as Moffat held Angel hostage with my Astra automatic, I wasn't going to do anything stupid. Perhaps he was frightened of the dark or holes in the rock.

I was glad to feel my feet touch firm ground, long before the length of rope ran out. I flicked the torch left and right and spotted a low tunnel opening.

"This way," I said, following the instructions I'd memorised from the parchment.

"I'm right behind you," Torres grunted.

"That's what the smell is, eh?" I said in English, but he didn't respond.

I ducked my head and entered the tunnel. It was about three feet wide and five feet high. Walking in a stooped position for thirty minutes was agonising on my back muscles. I just hoped it was as uncomfortable for Torres.

Then the tunnel opened into a cavern so vast our torches couldn't penetrate to its limits.

I straightened up and unkinked a few muscles in my neck and shoulders.

"Where now?" Torres pressed, his voice rebounding off the cavern walls. Slight skittering noises erupted high above, probably disturbed bats. He flinched at the sound and stared wide-eyed at me.

I sighed. "Just follow me. This way, but go carefully." I went on, ignoring him. He could either follow me or not, the choice was his.

Just ahead, a fallen stalactite formed a bridge over a seemingly bottomless chasm. It must have been there a few centuries. I clambered onto the stalactite and edged along its rough length. Fortunately, my soles had a good grip.

"Hey, wait for me!" Torres called.

I stopped and glanced over my shoulder, my torch beam in his face.

He put out an arm against the glare and I lowered the torch to illuminate the way across. He hurried, quick mincing steps on the stalactite surface, his arms out at either side to aid his balance.

"Don't rush," I warned, but I was too late.

Torres slipped on a mid-section that was damp from the drips of other limestone formations above. He overbalanced and slid off to the right.

I caught him in my torch beam as he fell, his shriek echoing then fading, as did he into the black oblivion below. I wondered if his cries had been heard up in the ruined windmill. I doubted it.

Time lost meaning down here. The air smelled damp, cloying. Perhaps there was an underground stream. I sniffed the air then coughed. I'd been in worse places. I followed the directions committed to memory. Deep underground as I was, I felt tense. Briefly, I wondered if another tremor might hit this area. I could be buried alive. I knew from experience that imagination was a double-edged sword: it developed caution and had saved my life more than once, but it also sent my heart hammering.

The final narrow defile was a tight fit for my build. Angel wouldn't have had any trouble squeezing through. An out-jutting rock scraped against my thigh and tore the trouser material, and then I was through.

My feet scrabbled on a slight incline, the sound echoing in the cavernous place. I let out an involuntary gasp.

Leon Cazador, P.I.

I'd made it. The torch illuminated the treasure. Some items were submerged under a wide pool of stagnant water, but most were littered around the festooned boulders and slabs of rock, probably thrown there during an old earthquake upheaval. Several timber chests were scattered among gold and silver figurines and candlesticks and glinted in the torch beam. Crosses, armour, shields, and dozens of embossed swords glinted back at me. My feelings were mixed. Naturally, I was excited. This was the first time I'd found lost treasure of any kind. But I felt sorry that Angel hadn't made the discovery first. I dragged my eyes from those riches. Beyond was a winding stone staircase.

I followed it upwards and gradually the air improved.

My watch told me it was about forty minutes later when I heaved my shoulders against the heavy stone of another trapdoor. Choking on dust and bits of soil, I hauled myself up into another rubble-strewn room. I was glad that no section of the ancient stone wall had collapsed to cover the trapdoor. I glanced around. Another building without a roof; with only one entrance. This one possessed a set of worn and crumbling stone steps leading up to what appeared to be battlements. Cautiously, I moved to the doorway and looked out. I smiled. I'd emerged in the base of the watchtower.

The fresh air was welcome. I gulped it down.

Kneeling, I retrieved from my ankle holster the lightweight Colt Officer's ACP LW automatic. The body search made by Torres had been perfunctory and he'd been lulled into false security when he found my Astra A-100 in its shoulder holster. "Some bodyguard you are," he'd said with a sneer.

Now I climbed the ancient steps and reached the top of the tower. Air gusted, reinvigorating. I crouched behind the parapet and methodically surveyed the land all round. From this vantage point, I looked down on the dilapidated windmill.

My heart missed a beat. Angel was lying down on his back, while Moffat kept pacing to and fro, one moment eyeing his watch, the next waving my automatic, all the while shouting at his archrival.

It was a long distance for an automatic. I stilled my anger and controlled my breathing, rested my gun-hand on the half collapsed battlement, aimed and fired.

I heard the .45 bullet *whang* off stone as the gun's report echoed in the gully.

Moffat stopped and hesitated. I could read him, all right. He glanced at the weapon in his hand, then at Angel. He toyed with using Angel as a hostage. I'd disabuse him of that idea.

I sent another bullet at him, closer this time. "You're surrounded!" I called, voice bouncing off the rocks and stone. He'd have no idea about my position.

Moffat didn't wait for Torres but threw the automatic on the ground. He wasn't a gunman. I was sure he had underlings to perform that kind of function. Besides, I was convinced he was a coward at heart. Moffat scrambled down the slope towards the abandoned dwellings.

I fired again, just to hasten his retreat.

***

When I got to Angel, he seemed in a bad way, his pallor quite gray. He struggled to sit up and leaned against a section of the windmill's old stone wall. His first words were, "You found it?"

I nodded and withdrew from my jacket pocket a gold cross and placed it in his trembling hand.

Tears welled. "My heart, old friend, it's giving up on me."

"Take it easy, Angel. The treasure can wait."

He shook his head. He wouldn't listen to me but went on, "You must use this treasure to fight men like Moffat."

"But it's treasure trove, Angel. It has historic value."

He winced, as if my words had been barbs in his flesh. "Ignorant people don't understand the value of history, Leon." His words were prophetic. Only last year Ecija excavations had uncovered an important Roman city, but the council had concreted over it for their car park.

"Sell the treasure to people who value it."

"I promise, Angel."

He clutched the cross to his chest and his eyes closed, a smile on his lips.

That was some years ago. I moved certain items to another site and Angel publicly "discovered" them there. That kept Moffat quiet for a while.

Angel lived comfortably for a few years more, content in the knowledge that he had achieved a lifetime's dream.

Leon Cazador, P.I.

I've hidden the rest of the treasure elsewhere. It helps to finance my forays against injustice and protect those innocent pilgrims in life beset by unprincipled men and women. I like to think that from time to time a few of the Knights Templar look down and approve.

Nik Morton

Leon Cazador, P.I.

NIGHT FISHING

Dusk fled quickly, as it does out here in the south of Spain. The warm night air was humid and still. The full moon's reflection glinted from the calm Mediterranean. Behind me, crickets *chirruped* but I barely heard them as I was concentrating on the little fishing boat out at sea, with its nightlight casting a circle of white around the stern. From the cliff top, I watched the three of them through 10x50 binoculars, and my fears were confirmed. Old Salvador Molina needed his strong sons to haul the net in because it seemed to contain a heavy object. My heart sank.

Sometimes, the night of unreason lurks in dark recesses, waiting to cloak the good earth, and it would seem that even this honest fisherman was not immune to the importuning of this evil night.

I had known old Salvador Molina for several years. He was hardworking and dedicated to his blind wife, Lucita. He barely managed to make a living from the sea. His two strapping sons, José and Luis, had left the family hearth to work in Alicante and sent money home whenever they could. Occasionally, though, the pair of them would join their father for a little night fishing.

Two weeks ago, Salvador came into some money. We all knew it wasn't lottery winnings, so it had to be an inheritance. We Spaniards have countless relatives. Not a single person in his village begrudged Salvador his good luck. Everyone said that now he could stay at home and look after Lucita.

But contrary to expectations, he didn't stay at home in his crumbling fishing cottage. Instead, he paid for it to be renovated and spent a great deal of time and patience showing Lucita where all the new furniture was so she wouldn't bump into it. His craggy features grew more lined with laughter and pleasure as he saw the joy these life changes wrought on Lucita's face.

Salvador bought a washing machine and a television that offered voice-over for blind viewers. But his greatest gift to his wife was the collection of talking books, which seemed to open up a whole new world for her. She was transported through her mind to foreign lands and ancient times.

Even though he didn't want for money and he was sixty-four, Salvador still went out night fishing, now with his two sons, who had moved back in following their family's good fortune.

Despite being by nature suspicious, I hadn't wanted to spy on them.

I hadn't wanted to see them pulling that package inboard, the water streaming off its plastic surface. I'd seen similar containers before: waterproofed boxes of cocaine.

Slowly, Salvador opened the seal and removed six packets, putting them into a careworn haversack that Luis held out. I breathed a slight sigh of relief. At least it wasn't cocaine. I recognised the shape of bank notes. A great deal of money. A bad deal, in fact.

The three of them continued casting their net for another hour, hauling in sufficient fish, doubtless to justify their night's outing.

When they dragged the boat ashore, their feet splashing in the small waves, I was waiting for them, trying to look nonchalant as I rested an arm on an oar and leaned against the upturned hull of a boat. All three stopped, clearly taken aback at my presence.

"Leon?" Salvador said, adjusting the haversack on his back. His two dark-haired sons stood on either side of him, fists clenched, eyes wary. Protective, threatening. All three wore canvas shoes, the toes sinking a little in the wet sand. "What are you doing here at this ungodly hour?"

"Ungodly is right, Salvador," I said. "I don't think you should be taking that bag home."

The two sons eyed each other, Luis nodded to José, and suddenly they both rushed me. Fortunately, I was prepared, grabbed the big oar and swung it round, bashing their knees and calves with it. Yelping in pain, they both tumbled to the sand and I stepped back, crouched and ready should they consider another attack.

My back was wet with that slight exertion, as the night was warm and humid.

Glaring at me, Salvador's sons struggled to their feet, hands dusting sand from their wet jeans.

I held up a hand. "I don't want to fight any of you," I said. "Just talk."

"Leave him!" Salvador barked. His drawn features were dark and shadowy, his cheeks sunken clefts. "This is no concern of yours, Leon."

I said, "Lucita doesn't know where the money has come from, does she?"

He stared at me with rheumy eyes but he couldn't hold my gaze. "No." He glanced down at his wet sand-covered canvas shoes. "*Madre de Dios*, you know, then?"

I nodded. "Yes."

He looked up, rubbed the back of his free hand against his bulbous nose and sniffed at a recollection. "It was just by chance." He gestured further up the coastline, towards Santa Pola. "My net got tangled in a line..." He let out a hoarse laugh. "Simple as that..."

"Nothing's that simple," I said. I dropped the oar but stood warily all the same, fists ready. "Some drug smugglers do that, Salvador. They attach lines and a weight and drop their boxes overboard and their floats are about two feet below the surface. As long as they've taken accurate bearings, they or their associates come back another time to retrieve the boxes. Payment—such as your little find—is made the same way."

Salvador nodded, briefly glanced out to sea then faced me. "I thought it was something like that." He shrugged again. "Surely they will not miss one box. They might think that it had broken loose from its line, no?"

"That's possible," I conceded. "But I believe you cut it loose and dragged it here and weighted it off-shore just below the surface, where you can get at it without hindrance. Your own little money bank."

"Those crooks," exclaimed Luis, "they will not miss one lousy box!"

I sighed and eyed Salvador. "How long is it since Lucita could see?"

"What has that got to do with anything?"

"Everything, Salvador. Everything."

His fingers rasped over his bristly chin as he considered my question. "She was blinded in the car crash eight years ago last month. But you know this..." He looked across at his two sons and the bright moonlight caught moisture on his eyelids. "A drunken driver, curse his bones!"

"Father, why are you talking to this man?" snarled José. "He has no right to question us. We can deal with him. Get rid of him."

"*Madre de Dios*, you will not speak like that! What would your mother say? You would shame me in front of Leon Cazador?"

"No, father, it is just..." José looked pleadingly at his brother but he gained no support as Luis screwed up his face in puzzlement.

"Silence, the pair of you!" Salvador turned to me. "What is your point, Leon? Make it quickly. It is late. Lucita, she will start to worry..."

"It is never too late, old friend. But think on this. There is little to choose between drug abuse and excessive alcohol. They both bring ruin and destroy families and friendships. Do you really believe that Lucita would be happy to know that she is benefiting from the money that causes so much misery?"

"But those drugs find their way onto the streets anyway!" Luis exclaimed. "It's only money, after all. It isn't as if it's drugs, is it?"

It is with such sophistry that the good are damned. "Two wrongs do not make a right, Luis." I gestured at them. "You know that and so does your father."

Salvador ran a hand down his face and groaned. "I have been an honest man all my life, as God is my witness. But when I realised what I had in my net, I–I..."

I grinned. "It must have been like winning *El Gordo*, old friend," I said. "But by using the dirty money you're not only condoning misery and death, you're endangering your family. If the drug smugglers ever found out that you had stolen their payment, they would show you and your family no mercy." I thrust into the dark recesses of my mind several images gleaned from past investigations. "No mercy," I emphasised.

Salvador eyed his sons, clearly distraught over his moral dilemma. "But it is already too late," he said, shrugging off the sack which now shook in his grasp. "We've spent so much already."

"As I said, it's never too late. Talk to my brother, Juan. He might see a way through all this."

***

It's useful having a brother in the *Guardia Civil*. My arrangements from time to time don't adversely affect his career either, since I help him bring crooks to justice.

Juan's two years older than me but has led a comparatively sheltered life, never having travelled abroad. Over the years, I'd built up quite a network of contacts in the various *Guardia* groups, a kind of symbiosis, which seemed to work.

Juan's intervention brought in two *Guardia Civil* special teams: the *Servicio Maritimo*, tasked with seashore surveillance, and the divers from the *Grupo Especial de Actividades Subacuáticas*. Salvador was able to help them by accurately pinpointing the position where he originally netted the waterproof container of bank notes.

The surveillance was into its fourth night. I watched from the cliff top with my brother and Salvador. Finally, Juan gripped my arm and whispered, "They're here!"

I raised the glasses and spotted the small boat chugging towards the spot Salvador had identified. Two men sat on the thwarts, automatic rifles slung over their shoulders, and a third in the stern steered the outboard. There wasn't even any pretence at fishing. In the fore end of the boat were several incriminating items: a waterproofed bundle, a weight and a small buoy.

Suddenly, the darkness was split with multiple searchlight beams from two *Guardia* boats to their left and right.

A megaphone blared, the voice echoing: "Surrender, this is the *Guardia Civil,* and we have our weapons trained on you!"

I saw one of the men fumble with the package, about to throw it overboard, but he desisted as two sharp shots hit the water at the boat's side. The man at the tiller started to turn the boat in a curve, as if to head out to sea, but more shots dissuaded him and he cut the motor.

The two *Guardia* vessels closed, armed *guardia* lining the sides.

It was quite a haul. The bundle contained six kilos of cocaine. The arrested men eventually admitted that they were scheduled to pick up the money in payment for the drugs. No, they couldn't say who had placed the payment.

In the official announcement of the drug bust, mention was made that there was no money at the drop off spot. It was hoped that this would have two immediate effects: Whoever left the money would distrust the drug traffickers, and the drug merchants would suspect their client of double dealing and mete out their own form of "justice".

The question of the dirty money—that paid for the renovation of an old cottage, a television, a washing machine and talking books—was conveniently forgotten.

Sometimes, there are shades of gray in the world. Lucita never learned the truth about Salvador's 'windfall'. A few months later, the local hospital and school benefited from an anonymous benefactor.

Salvador no longer goes night fishing and keeps his wife company while their sons have returned to Alicante to work.

However, I still go night fishing. Fishing for evil men. Because I believe that bringing the ungodly to justice helps to hold back the encroaching night of unreason.

Leon Cazador, P.I.

ADOPTED COUNTRY

On a clear day like today, I felt I could almost reach out and touch Africa. I stood alongside my brother, Juan, on the seashore of Tarifa, Spain's southernmost tip. Juan was the *Guardia Civil* officer supervising the capture of yet another boatload of illegal immigrants.

Earlier, squinting out to sea as the *Guardia Civil* launch intercepted the over-laden longboat, Juan had said, "It isn't surprising, Leon, is it? North Africa is only fourteen kilometres away from where we stand. They want an easier and better life here in Europe so they'll risk everything in the attempt."

"No, Juan, it isn't surprising."

Now, I watched with a heavy heart as medical teams and officials, flanked by Juan's men, swooped on the women, men and children who clambered wearily from the beached vessel. The area was ring-fenced with police carrying machine guns.

It was a motley collection of humanity: pregnant women with hypothermia, children whose ribcages were visible through the taut skin, and once-strong lithe men with exhausted faces and wary eyes. A short distance, but often a treacherous journey. Even though they were staring down the barrels of guns, these were the lucky ones. Countless people died making the crossing every year. Desperation does that.

Since my country's agreement with Morocco and the erection of barbed wire along the common border, it is now virtually impossible to enter Spain through the Ceuta route. So thousands go further along the North African coast and pay their entire savings to board any old boat that will sail for Tarifa or some other beach along the southern coast of Spain. Thousands even attempt the seven hundred mile crossing to the Canary Islands, and many more perish in the attempt.

Sadly, over forty years of independence hasn't made the African nations a better and safer place to live. All kinds of bloodletting conflict has left the land poorer and thrust millions on the asylum-seeking trail. Only last week I'd seen the refugee camp in the inhospitable dry south of Morocco. It was populated with people from the Congo, the Ivory Coast, Liberia, and Sierra Leone, among others. These dreamers of a decent life faced being beaten up, locked up, humiliated, over-exploited and even killed. And yet they considered the risk worth it.

For every illegal immigrant burglar and mugger Spain suffers, there are at least fifty illegal immigrants working all the hours of daylight in the avocado, banana and other high-yield farms. Moroccans rub shoulders with Ecuadoreans and Colombians, forever glancing over their shoulders for the police, fearing the very real threat of arrest and deportation.

Beside us was parked a *Guardia Civil* prisoner van with its strong grille windows. Inside sat one man, half-naked and sullen. This was the man I'd hoped to find today. Mehdi al-Hadidi.

Juan sighed, voicing how I felt as I turned to watch the ambulances and trucks take all of the others away. We both stared at the tire tracks on the wet sand.

"It isn't their fault they were displaced by a blood-lusting dictator, is it?" Juan asked.

"There is no easy answer," I said. "But the social system is already straining under the weight of EU migrants." I shook my head, wondering what the future held for Europe.

Clambering up beside the prison van driver, Juan said, "The answer surely lies in improving the African countries, ridding them of the deadly corruption. I know there's corruption everywhere, especially in the EU, but it doesn't lead to genocide and displacing millions of people, it doesn't create deserts out of arable land. Zimbabwe is just the worst example, the breadbasket of Africa turned into a basket case."

"Tell that to some of our developers!" I said bitterly. "They're buying up farm land at an alarming rate, even though the boom has come to an end with the credit crunch."

"Don't go cynical on me, brother." He shut the door and leaned out the open window. "If their lives were simple and decent without fear of death, if their countries were desirable again, they wouldn't want to risk everything to come north where it is colder and far from welcoming."

"True enough, I suppose," I admitted, moving to the back of the truck. "Yet evil men are quite content to treat cynically with the impoverished to further their dark ends."

Mehdi al-Hadidi glared at me through the grille, his dark eyes glinting with an unfathomable fanaticism. In my fairly long and varied life, I've met more than my fair share of fanatics and evil men and women. Even so, my spine went cold as I studied him.

***

A week earlier, I helped break up an al-Qaeda terrorist cell in Torrevieja. It wasn't the first of its kind, nor would it be the last, though perhaps these deranged murderers would think twice about setting up shop in this area. There were forty officers involved and five suspects were arrested—three Algerians and two Moroccans. Three houses and two commercial units were searched, netting twenty kilos of cocaine, a variety of weapons, false documents and €15,000 in cash.

Several leads that I'd picked up from a few reliable contacts had pointed to the terrorists' address, so I was allowed to go on the raid in an unofficial capacity. Having friends in high places helped, too. My time in Intelligence on the Spanish Embassy staff proved useful.

I studied the five suspects, each one wearing plastic handcuffs and sitting on the floor with his back to the wall of the bedroom. The Moroccan, Bouthayna Tassi, seemed the weakest of them. I'd been around enough to recognise the traits. It's mainly in the eyes, but also the body language. Hard to define, but gut instinct told me he was my best option. I was given ten minutes, which enabled me to ask a few pertinent questions of Tassi.

These people are not pleasant. The majority are cowards. They're quite content to brainwash their form of cannon fodder while skulking in shadows, killing innocents by remote, all in the name of a truly warped view of a great religion.

It only took me five minutes to convince Tassi to tell me what I'd come here to find out. Possibly, my methods of persuasion would be frowned upon in a civilised society, but in my heart of hearts, I took no pleasure in extracting the information.

"I will visit you in the compound if you lie to me," I promised him.

"She, she is where I say. Believe me, infidel!"

I'd taken on the case for peanuts, which was just as well, as my client could barely afford to buy nuts to live. Buchi Mutebule was a Congolese asylum seeker who had arrived in Spain a month ago, then vanished. Now Tassi reluctantly told me that she'd been sold to an al-Qaeda group who used her to earn money.

Nothing new there, then. It happened all the time. Trade in sex, booze and drugs was nothing to them. Their religion, so it went, allowed them to transgress if it saved their lives or furthered their cause. Something like that, anyway. Pure hypocrisy.

Tassi admitted that illegal drug sales and the trade of counterfeit DVDs also financed his group, the latter unwittingly purveyed by compliant Chinese.

Slavery may be abolished, but it's alive and well in the twenty-first century in so-called civilised Europe.

***

Alone, I followed Tassi's directions and found the house on an *urbanización* quite close to Guardamar del Segura. I placed myself behind a graffiti-daubed electricity substation building and settled down to observe.

The detached building was called a villa by estate agents, but it was little more than a two-bedroom bungalow. It looked abandoned and weeds grew round the empty swimming pool. Behind the black metal grilles, the *persianas* were down. Four steps went up to the entrance patio. The heavy dark oak front door's varnish peeled.

The place looked no different than other forlorn residences abandoned at the time of the financial crisis. There was neither a SE ALQUILA nor a SE VENDE notice in evidence. Maybe the owner had died, or thrown himself off a twenty-storey building like an honourable financial whiz kid full of remorse. As if.

I carried my trusty Astra A-100 automatic. Made in Spain. It felt comfortable and reassuringly heavy in my hand and I was glad of the fifteen 9mm parabellum rounds it held, as Tassi said there could be four or five men living here at any one time.

After watching the place for two hours, checking the back and the front, I detected no movement in the villa. Then at last, I noticed a man sauntering towards the gate. He was a short Asian and wore blue striped *piratas*, flip-flops and a badly creased off-white T-shirt. He held a carryout bag from the nearby Chinese restaurant, and it looked as though the contents might feed two or three at a pinch.

The man opened the gate—it creaked on rusty hinges—and walked up the cracked path to the entrance steps. He stood on the porch, fishing one-handed for a key. Once he'd found it, he glanced up and down the street then turned and inserted the key. He pushed open the door.

When I have to, I can move very quickly indeed. Before he could close the door behind him, I'd vaulted over the gate, raced up the steps and shoulder-barged the door.

He stumbled backwards and yelped. But he retained his grip on the food.

I leveled my automatic and snapped, "Quiet. ¡*Silencio!*"

Standing in the centre of the unfurnished lounge, his eyes widened, intent on the pistol. Hurriedly, he nodded.

Careful to keep the man covered, I checked him out. In his trouser pocket, he was carrying a small black Russian pistol, the PSM, its 5.45mm shells capable of penetrating body armour. These nasty weapons were freely available on the black market in Central Europe but have since found their way to Spain.

I forced him to lead me through the lounge to the bedroom door at the rear. It was locked, but I soon persuaded him to open it. I shoved him inside and flicked on the lights. He fell against the bottom of a metal bedstead, and the Chinese food spilled out of the bag.

Chained to the bed head were three women, and in the centre, I recognised Buchi from her photo. They were all quite thin. The whites of their eyes showed terrible fear as all three noticed my automatic.

At that moment, I was sorely tempted to shoot the man, their captor.

"Buchi, I'm a friend of your brother, Kissanga," I explained, stepping forward and clubbing the man's temple with the gun butt. He slumped unconscious into the spilled chow mein.

"Kissanga, he's alive?" she exclaimed, joy lighting up her face.

"Yes, he obtained asylum and never once believed you had died on the boat."

The two women with Buchi were Moroccan and, as soon as I freed them, they were only too happy to divulge a great deal of interesting information.

Nowadays, illegal immigrants slipped into Spain through the airports on short term work or holiday visas, and of course never left. But al-Qaeda knew that the airports were watched. So, for over a year they'd been sending their best fanatics over among the boatpeople.

The two women told me how they'd overheard their five captors talking, boasting.

And that was how I heard about Mehdi al-Hadidi and his attempt to enter Spain as an illegal immigrant with those who were genuinely fleeing oppression.

Once we were expecting him, it had been easy enough to identify al-Hadidi. After all, compared to the others, he was well fed. And now he was on his way to Madrid, charged as a suspected terrorist.

***

Throughout history, immigrants have brought diversity, language, skills and culture to their adopted countries. And compassion dictates that we should deal fairly with refugees. But now is the time of economic migrants—and terrorist infiltrators. Compassion is wearing thin under these new threats to national identity, stability and security.

Maybe my brother was right, after all. Perhaps the affluent nations should be doing more about the poor countries. Easier said than done, though. The problem was too immense to contemplate, it seemed to me. The exodus from Africa would not be stemmed until that continent's five wants were adequately met: basic food, water, sanitation, education, and freedom from tyranny.

For now, though, I would have to console myself that at least I was able to reunite a brother and sister. Perhaps they would be able to find gainful employment and enjoy their new lives in their adopted country, Spain.

Leon Cazador, P.I.

GRAVE CONCERNS

The mass grave by the roadside was not the first in Spain to be unearthed in the last four years, and it wouldn't be the last. On each side were carobs and bright yellow and blue wild flowers, a tranquil contrast to the macabre sight before us. Men in the trench wore gauze masks over their mouths as they lifted out human bones and strips of clothing and placed them reverently on a length of tarpaulin. Behind them stood an idle mechanical earth-digger, while beyond the fields of rosemary and artichokes rose the rugged mountains, mute witnesses to what had happened about sixty-seven years ago.

I stood and watched while Clara Landera sat beside me on a green plastic chair by the edge of the road. She was in her seventies and wore the traditional black clothing of constant mourning and, despite the heat of the day, a black woollen shawl crossed her chest and was tucked into her black skirt's waistband. Her thick dark stockings were wrinkled, like her face. Mascara encircled Clara's old eyes, rouge emphasised her sunken cheeks, and her lips were painted carmine.

As I placed a heavy hand on her shoulder, her rough palm patted my knuckles. "I have no tears left to shed," she murmured.

I understood. For many years, I'd known her as Clara Marzal until one dark evening she explained her tragic past. She had been sitting on her balcony, smoking a cigarillo, watching the television through her window. The screen showed a news item about the digging up of a Civil War mass grave. As the bottle of white wine emptied, her story gradually poured out.

***

While a new conflict raged across the world, the old Civil War that ended in Spring 1939 still claimed many lives. The reprisals of el Caudillo and his extreme right-wing followers killed thousands of *los rojos*—the Communists. Nothing was said about the illegal executions and the abduction of children from their families.

Clara's pueblo was like so many, riven by fanatics of the left and the right. The Civil War was anything but civil, it was barbaric. Old wounds were reopened and old scores were settled with bloodletting on both sides.

In the dead of night in 1940, five men, three women and two children were taken away in a truck by village Falangists. Clara was one of the children and her mother Jacinta was with her. After a short drive, they stopped and were told to get out. Clara was forced to watch as the men in their blue shirts and leather webbing shot her mother, her grandparents and the others. To this day Clara could not wear anything coloured blue as it brought back the memories. The bodies were dumped unceremoniously into a ditch overgrown with weeds. An arm and hand stuck out, and Clara was convinced it was her mother, waving goodbye.

Nothing was done for over half a century. It was a conspiracy of silence born of fear. Even after the *transición* to democracy, the questioning voices were stilled.

With the new millennium, however, some individuals began to claim their family's dead. They wanted them properly laid to rest.

"I cried with pain. And hate." Clara had most of her own teeth and clenched her jaw tightly. "I may have been only four, but I have remembered all the names of those murderers." She gripped her rosary beads. "Now, before I go the way of all flesh, I want my mother's remains put in her final resting place."

When I drove her to the spot that had figured in her nightmares until she was a teenager, Clara was surprised how little had changed. Inland Spain was timeless, it seemed, compared with the raped overdeveloped coast. Long may that be so.

We laid a wreath and on my return, I kept my promise to Clara and set in motion the paperwork for the disinterment of the bodies she claimed lay there.

***

Months later, at the reburial, few witnesses attended. Many villagers didn't want to know. Some had died, never knowing the truth. Others were not interested in raking over the past. "Let it lie," they said.

Pedro Jarillo was not one of those. He welcomed this solemn closure. He was in his eighty-ninth year and there was a haunted look about him, as if he could already feel the icy finger of his mortality on his shoulder. His bowed shape was slightly aloof, at the side of the small number of mourners.

The hearse made its way into the *cementerio*, a handful of people in black walking behind.

Instead of gravestones and the solitary Victorian tombs of England, this final resting place resembled a tiny town: the streets of the dead, complete with lamps and paved paths. Instead of doors and windows, there were square stone or marble niches, decorated with flowers, epigrams, religious tableaux, the Virgin Mary, Jesus, or photographs of the deceased. They were five tiers high, like elaborate filing cabinets. Whenever I visited a cemetery, I was reminded of the many mortuaries I'd been in, their cadavers lying in drawers.

As the hearse stopped at the empty vacant niche, second up from the ground, two men in overalls stepped round a corner, puffing on thick cigars. They carried a pail each and deposited them to one side, then removed the coffin from the hearse and eased it into its niche, while the readings from Lorca accompanied the mortal remains of Clara's mother on her last journey.

Then the two men set to work. They placed the stone slab over the hole and plastered it secure.

Clara strode purposefully up to Pedro and suddenly slapped his face. The sound rebounded off the walls of the surrounding graves. She turned on her heel and walked away, leaving loud whispers and murmurings of displeasure behind her.

***

I stood on Pedro Jarillo's doorstep. As he opened the heavy oak door, I said, "You asked to see me."

He nodded, let me in and closed the door behind me. The room was cool and sombre, furnished with dark wood and leather, and it smelled old, like him.

"I know you are a friend of Clara," he said, and ruefully stroked his unshaved cheek, making a rasping sound.

"Yes." I hesitated, but realised there was no other way to say it, except outright: "She told me you and your father were there with the other Falangists that night."

He sighed deeply, as if letting out in that single action, years of dread and guilt. "Yes, so help me, I was." He pointed at a timeworn leather sofa, and I lowered myself into it. He sat on a ladder-backed chair, shoulders hunched, forearms resting on his knees as he faced me.

His eyes were pale with age now but probably had been shining bright brown when he was a young man. In years gone by, he must have been handsome, a catch for any girl. He made a helpless gesture. "Many of those men who were with me have died. Whether among the dead or the living, they never had any regrets. They believed that what they did was necessary. They justified themselves, saying *los rojos* had committed crimes just as bad."

"Two wrongs don't make a right, though, do they?"

"No," he said firmly, "they don't. Ever."

I nodded. "But you do have regrets, is that it?"

"Already, you sound like my confessor, Señor Cazador."

"No, but I am a good listener," I said. "Tell me, Pedro Jarillo. Tell me why you cannot face speaking to Clara."

Even though his recall was surprisingly detailed, it took a while in the telling.

Pedro's father was one of the area's Falangist leaders, short in stature and temper, with constant stubble on his face and small penetrating dark eyes. He was acting on a recent denunciation that stated their prospective prisoners had been Republican sympathisers during the Civil War. Like many in his position, he never questioned the credibility of the denunciation or the relationship of the people involved. Old enmities and jealousies were not considered relevant. "We have to be seen to be strong," he told his twenty-two-year-old son.

All the way to the home of the Landera family, Pedro had fretted, his insides like jelly. He knew what they were going to do. His mouth was dry, and his heart ached. No matter how he felt about it, he couldn't back out and bring shame to his father.

Shame had already cast its bleak shadow on Señor and Señora Landera since their simpleton daughter, Jacinta, had become pregnant. The village castigated them for neglecting poor unmarried Jacinta. "The Landera *puta* is not worthy of the blessing of a child," some said. Others declaimed the morals of the young in general. Jacinta gave birth to Clara, and she was a delightful healthy child adored by all, even those critical of her family. No amount of goading, beatings or threats of eternal damnation would convince Jacinta to reveal the name of the little girl's father.

On that dark night, the Landera family and others who had been denounced were forced into the back of a truck. Tears and pleas fell on deaf ears.

Pedro briefly put his hands over his ears, but it made no difference. He tried to turn his heart and mind to stone, but failed. It was not right!

As they drove behind the truck containing Jacinta, Clara, and the others, Pedro finally blurted out, "Father, little Clara, she is my daughter!"

"*Madre de Dios*!" His father nearly crashed their car into the back of the truck. He swore, and his big fist smashed down on the steering wheel. "They were Republicans, Pedro!" He turned to face his son, his eyes fiery, glaring. "Look what they did to the village of Segura del Carmen! They must pay!"

"But, Father, she is only a child."

"*Madre de Dios*!" growled his father, moving the car forward again. "The shame of it!"

The rest of the journey took about five minutes, but in that time Pedro's father had resolved what they would do.

It was dark as everyone stepped down from the vehicles.

Swiftly and unseen, Pedro appeared from behind the truck and grabbed Clara and broke her mother's grip on the girl's little hand. Before she could shout out, he covered Clara's mouth with his palm, almost smothering the poor child.

Jacinta screamed but nobody paid her any attention. They had expected hysterics from her anyway.

The men and women and a child were shoved along in single-file further up the road, full in the beam of the truck's headlights.

Then they were told to stop and turn with their backs to the ditch.

The priest stepped out of another car and took their confessions.

They were all brave, even Jacinta, who had gone very quiet.

As he had promised his father, Pedro forced little Clara to watch.

When it was all over, he carried her over his shoulder and hid with her in the back of his father's car.

"We will go to the convent of Santa Teresa," his father said when he got in. "They can look after her. Though I fear she is damned."

***

"Does Clara know you are her father?" I asked.

"My God, no." Pedro shook his head, his eyes evading mine. "As much as I wanted to, I couldn't save her mother. I left the village for many years and never spoke to my father until he was on his deathbed. All this time, wherever I travelled, I have been unable to forgive myself."

I leaned forward and put a hand on his shoulder.

His body trembled, shaking with an old grief, but still he stared down at the tiled floor.

"Look at me, Pedro," I said.

He raised his head, and I feared that the light of life in his eyes was almost extinguished.

"You know what happened, of course," I said. "Your daughter became Clara Marzal, the famous actress and singer."

He nodded. "Yes, despite everything, she made something of her life."

"It's more than that, Pedro. She used her pain to inform her acting and songs."

"Yes, I have heard her sing. More than once she has made me cry. I don't know if it's because of the words of her songs or the fact that I never knew her, never watched her grow up." He shook his head, his fist pressing against his chest. "I ache, knowing what I have missed and what I haven't been able to give her."

"You don't have to forgive yourself. That's up to her. Give her this chance."

He raised a hand to the cheek she'd slapped. "But—"

"Remind her that, at great risk to yourself, you saved her life."

***

As I watched the two old people standing on the bridge over the dry *rio*, I could see that their eyes were not dry.

I don't know what they said, but they shook hands and both seemed reluctant to let go. It was a beginning.

Leon Cazador, P.I.

FAIR COP

Fairs bring out the best and the worst in some people. Today was Torre del Pozo's annual *feria*. Perched a kilometre from the rugged rocks and sand dunes, the village was awash with colourful ribbons, flags and banners. The main street was closed off by police barriers and lined on either side by stalls. Near the *ayuntamiento* and church was a fenced and straw-filled arena where livestock would be sold. As I sat at an outside café table and sipped my second *cortado* of the day, the air was filled with the cries of cocks, the clucking of hens and the lowing of cattle. The fireworks would come later. If my informant was correct, and he usually was, today I would catch one of the most elusive among the ungodly.

I waved to an old Scottish lady, Mrs. Forsyth, who was visiting from the neighbouring *urbanización*, Puente Tonel de los Pozos, which the *extranjeros* affectionately called Tunbridge.

Mrs. Forsyth smiled and nodded her head at a tall balding man wearing a tight T-shirt that showed off his tattooed forearms. Rodney Gridge was Mrs. Forsyth's neighbour. He often made her life unpleasant, drinking and shouting until the early hours. It was an open secret that he boasted about claiming disability benefits from his home country. He supplemented the payments from the Ministry of Work and Pensions with cash-in-hand jobs, such as laying roofs and painting exterior walls.

If he hadn't been so arrogant about it, perhaps Gridge would have got away with fleecing his country's taxpayers. However, as Mrs. Forsyth's unhappiness came to my notice, I decided to redress the balance. I detest cheats and bullies. My friend, José Antonio, photographed Gridge working on a few rooftops and these images accompanied a report which was on its way to the appropriate department at Newcastle-Upon-Tyne. I smiled, remembering that half my childhood barrio had supported that great soccer team. I gave Mrs. Forsyth the thumbs-up sign, signifying that Gridge's comeuppance was imminent.

The official presence of the *policia local* was Jesus Fernandez, who wore designer sunglasses. I know he recognised me, but he didn't acknowledge me. He idly moved to the north of the street and I followed. His plain-clothes associate, Chico, also wearing Ray-Bans, walked south.

Families congregated on both sides of the main street. Old ladies jostled for the chairs at the front, all the better to bounce their grandchildren on their knees while watching the procession and band. At the head of the pageant walked the mayor and his wife, accompanied by his family members and friends, all of whom had been suitably rewarded with positions in the town's administration. Then came the priest and, behind him, the effigy of the Holy Madonna carried by burly men in black. Another carved statue came next, San Fermín, the town's patron saint. The saint was followed by women and children waving gaudy banners embroidered with the well-tower emblem of the town.

Aside from the full turnout of townspeople, there were over a hundred foreigners, though I imagine not all were actually tourists. A good few were probably residents keen to absorb the local culture. Despite the country's countless transformations over the last three decades, it seemed that the real Spain would not change. And for that, I was thankful.

I noticed her as a group of tourists sauntered from stall to stall. She wasn't interested in the wares and only had eyes for the man's zip-up pouch on his belt. She wore black—a diaphanous scarf, a long dress and a bolero top over a cotton blouse. Black eyebrows that met over a broad nose and dark eyes did not suggest a disposition of sweetness and light. She expertly edged the zip open, a little fingertip movement at each step that the unwary tourist made. I moved closer, but I was in a quandary because she wasn't my quarry today, and I didn't want to give myself away. But I couldn't allow her to steal, either.

At the very instant when she opened the pouch entirely and her fingers were inside, I stepped forcefully on her foot and didn't budge. She made an involuntary movement and her mark finally realised what she was up to. "Bloody 'ell," he said, "she was in my pouch!" Strange, what we say in extremis.

The woman couldn't move and, lips curling, glared at me. If I believed in such things, a dark spell had just been cast in my direction. I was more concerned about keeping a wary eye on her hands, in case she had a knife. Unlike some market thieves, she worked alone and had no nearby accomplice to whom she could pass on her booty.

"Oh, *perdón, Señora*." As I moved my foot off hers, Jesus clamped a hand on her shoulder and advised her to accompany him.

Her intended victim laughed. "Bloody 'ell, it's the police! Great stuff!"

As Jesus and the Brit talked about making out a denunciation, I melted into the crowd.

A few feet ahead, a small cluster of people gathered—ideal fodder for pickpockets. I hastily scanned the rear of the group but couldn't identify any known dips.

Acting interested in what was happening, I moved closer and saw a foldaway cardboard table and the three thimbles: the shell game, perpetrated for centuries, and yet it still caught people unawares. It was illegal, but they stationed lookouts to avoid arrest.

"I'm quick with the pea, no mistake," the operator said. His mouth smiled but his eyes didn't, as they were very active, scrutinising the onlookers and doubtless keeping a watch on his lookouts. He spoke Spanish since very few there were foreign. Made a change, I thought. Often the most gullible are the Brits who think they can best the man. Nobody beats the shell man, the operator.

"But if you keep an eye out," said the operator, "you *can* beat me." As he spoke, he popped the single pea under a thimble and moved the three thimbles around.

I knew which thimble the pea was under.

"It's a fair game," he said. And so it appeared. But appearances can be deceiving.

A young woman standing at the front laughed. "That's easy. I know where it is!" Tall and attractive, she was from northern Spain with the fair colouring from her Celtic ancestors. Her fair hair was tied back in a chignon. She wore a fetching white top and her black bra was visible through the material. Her jeans hugged a narrow waist and ample hips. She pointed to the same thimble that I had mentally selected.

The operator shook his head, taunting. "Do you want to bet?"

"Yes! I'm feeling lucky!"

A €5 note changed hands. When the thimble was lifted, of course the pea wasn't there but under another one. Sleight-of-hand. Even when you know how it works, the switch is often made while money is handed over or some other minor distraction occurs. You never see the operator moving the pea.

I left the operator to his patter. He would let the young woman win once in a while, but she would end up losing in the end.

The loud-speaker announced that the *paella* was coming along nicely and anyone who wanted to add a rabbit to the mix had better hop to it, though I don't think they intended any pun.

As I eased through the crowd, I detected the middle-aged man who was working with the operator. In fact, he was there to bet and lose and sometimes win to encourage the onlookers to take part. In shell-game parlance, he was the shill.

Two identified, but where were the lookouts?

Then I spotted them. The one to the north was a young man, about fifteen. I hadn't noticed him earlier as he'd been slacking on the job and chatting up a pretty señorita in a red and white flamenco dress. But now he was watching over the heads of the people. Uniforms would send up the alarm and scare the pea-men off. The lookout to the south was a tall middle-aged man with designer stubble. His height allowed him to spot any encroaching police, but he never saw Chico coming. I nodded and Chico pounced, handcuffing the man to a stall's metal upright before he could flinch. I glanced in the other direction, and the pretty woman in the flamenco dress handcuffed the teenager.

Satisfied, I joined the watching group again. It wouldn't take the operator long to realise his lookouts were out of action.

As the fair-haired young woman placed her next bet, I sidled up behind the shill and whispered in his ear, "You're under arrest."

He froze for a moment then swung round with a clenched fist. But it didn't connect. I sidestepped and slapped a handcuff on his outstretched arm and followed up by ducking and yanking his arm down with me and securing the other cuff to his ankle. He lost his balance and toppled over. Some people laughed at his discomfiture, not really appreciating what was going on.

At that same moment, fair-haired Carlotta Diaz slammed her hand down on the thimble in the centre and pulled out the pea, holding it between finger and thumb. "I win!" she exclaimed as the table collapsed and all those watching applauded.

The operator stared in disbelief. I suspect that his pride wouldn't permit him to run off. The look on his face told me that he had never been beaten.

Carlotta walked over the collapsed table and handcuffed the operator. "By the way," she added, "you're nicked."

On the flattened cardboard table were the three upset thimbles and a pea.

Carlotta turned to me and winked, tossing her own pea in the air.

Nik Morton

Leon Cazador, P.I.

BITTER ALMONDS

"You know, Leon," Arturo Martinez said three weeks ago, "even with the water shortage, it looks like my crop's going to be all right."

I thought he was luckier than many fellow almond growers further north, like Xixona, for example, where there were real worries about desertification of the soil.

He was proud of his *hectares* of almond trees that he'd nurtured since inheriting them from his father twenty years before.

Arturo was a man of the earth in every sense. Not for him the trappings of modern wealth. I sometimes berated him over his wife, Carmen, using an old top-loader washtub and mangle. "She isn't getting any younger," I said, though I'm sure she wouldn't thank me for saying so. "Surely you can afford to buy her a new appliance and save her all that drudgery!"

Face deeply lined by the winds and browned by the sun, he shook his head. "Our wealth is in our land." His dark eyes sparkled in the half light of the late evening. "Besides, she has told me time and again she doesn't want any of those new-fangled contraptions!"

Then his chest inflated. "True, we are probably worth almost €60,000 on paper. But I'm at the bottom end, the producer. The markets make the big profits. Yes, we make money and could live comfortably with what is in the bank, if we were careful, but I put much of it back into our land."

Their son Rafael would inherit as Arturo had, though he wasn't keen on working on the land and instead was quite content to sit in front of a computer in a Benidorm office. Many farmers' children were fleeing the agricultural land. That land, in turn, was being sold to the ubiquitous developers and builders. Arturo knew all this, of course, but didn't dwell on it. As far as he was concerned, land was on loan anyway, as was, in the final analysis, all life.

What mattered to Arturo was how you treated the land, how you lived your life.

Grinning wickedly, his dark eyes glinting, he added, "Mind you, every six months I take my Carmen for a break in Barcelona. We have a good time, and we're up singing and dancing all hours. Lately, I must admit my legs seem to groan and creak more than is comfortable. And I still fret about leaving my almonds to the tender mercies of Emilio, my good neighbour. Yet when I return, it is always fine."

We sat on a dry stone wall, surveying the sweep of his land.

To most people, it seemed surprising that so many trees could find sustenance from what appeared to be unpromising dry earth. It required hard work, a knowledge gleaned over many years, much discipline and a strong back, particularly as Arturo never bothered with mechanisation.

His almonds, he said, were the best in the region.

A *Guardia Civil* helicopter flew at the southern extremity of his land.

Arturo pointed. "Chasing illegals, eh?"

I shook my head. "No, not this time, my friend."

Two reliable informants had mentioned to me that a small cannabis farm was flourishing in a *barranco* next to Arturo's land. I passed on that was why I was visiting, really. I told him this.

"They are fools, to take drugs."

I shrugged. "We all drink wine and coffee. And many smoke."

"You don't lose your sense of who you are, what you can be, with coffee and cigarettes," he said. He returned my shrug. "Wine, well, that's a little different, it depends on the individual. Moderation is best, Leon. I only drink a bottle a day!"

The helicopter dipped behind a crest of land. The arrests would happen shortly.

Our conversation lapsed into one of those companionable silences between friends.

The last time I'd been here was in February when the trees were in full blossom. Arturo's family had planted two varieties of tree, as the almond isn't self-pollinating. And to help with the pollination they'd also set up a series of beehives. When the blossom was out, it was a contest between the crickets and the bees as to which was the loudest. The sound of nature at work was strangely settling.

Abruptly, Arturo's head jerked round. "Can you hear that?" His tone was urgent.

My ears were sullied by too much living in towns and cities, but after a moment I heard it, too—a horrible sharp cracking sound.

I'd heard it before and so had Arturo.

"¡*Madre de Dios*, it's a fire!"

A shift in the evening breeze brought the unmistakeable smell of burning wood and vegetation, scented with almonds.

"My home!" Arturo shouted, jumping off the wall. "Dear God, Carmen!"

Much earlier, while Carmen busied herself in the kitchen preparing a meal for the three of us, Arturo and I had strolled up this gentle rise in his fields to take in the view. Now the view was vanishing behind clouds of smoke as we ran back down.

We were both out of breath by the time we got to the imposing entrance. "No matter how small your house, you must have an entrance arch to be proud of," Arturo once said.

The fire was raging about twenty yards behind his house. It had come from the adjoining land, near the roadside. As he rushed inside, I got my old Seat started.

Seconds later, he hurried out, hand-in-hand with Carmen who was clutching a leather photo album to her ample chest.

"Quickly, get inside!" I urged, opening the car doors.

I bundled them in, ignoring Carmen's entreaties about her belongings and her apologies about the aborted meal. "I fear it will be overcooked before long."

There were a few hairy moments, as some trees seemed to explode on either side of us, shooting nut cases like bullets at the windscreen. The glass was starred but survived intact. Nothing much else did, though.

The fire raged for hours. Arturo was ruined. His livelihood, his precious almond trees, his home —everything gone. He had Carmen and that was all.

Try as she did, Carmen couldn't seem to pull him out of his dark trough of despair.

I checked back with the *guardia* and asked to view their helicopter video footage. We were in luck. These days, they video any raid they make. Fortunately, they switched on the camera early and on the bottom left-hand corner of the screen we could see the youths running away from their out-of-control barbeque, clambering into their camper van and driving off. The enhanced picture identified their vehicle registration.

They were Madrileños, criminally oblivious to the dangers of lighting fires or throwing cigarettes out of car windows during a drought.

I sensed that it would be a difficult case to prosecute, and the only people who would benefit would be the lawyers.

***

Leaving the broken shell of a man, my friend Arturo, I called on Señor Escobar, the wealthy father of the main culprit. A manservant showed me into the foyer of the Escobar family's Madrid mansion. The marble and iron staircase rose majestically to a landing with a balcony.

After a moment, Señor Escobar stepped out of a room that was lined with books and shook my hand. "A terrible business, Señor Cazador." His voice tended to echo in the lobby. He had a hooked nose and steely-gray eyes.

He led me into the study and we sat beside a tall bay window. "What can I do for you?"

I explained. No amount of money could restore the most precious things they had lost. It wasn't about Rafael's inheritance, either, because he'd eventually get the insurance payout.

"In his heart my friend knows your son and his pals didn't mean to cause the fire," I ended.

"It was a careless act," Escobar said. "Two or three seconds of inattention, then, *whoosh*!" He sighed. "My Paco, the young, they don't consider the consequences of their actions." He shook his head. "Your friend must be utterly devastated."

I nodded. "Señor Martinez is ailing. He needs his belief in human nature to be restored."

"I think I understand." He stood up and crossed over to his writing desk and opened a drawer. He took out a chequebook. "How much?"

I shook my head. "He would only consider your money, however generously offered, as charity."

"I see, Señor Cazador. Leave it with me."

***

Arturo's will to live seemed barely a flicker, but Carmen kept that flame alight as they stayed with cousins in the nearby town.

Finally, the time had come, and I took them both back to their charred land.

Arturo stood with the aid of a walking stick and Carmen's strong arm.

Even after a couple of weeks, the smell of burnt almonds still lingered.

"What's happening here?" Arturo asked. There were many people in the fields; their faces smudged black with the embers.

"They're from the village," I said. "They've come to help."

"Help?" Arturo said gruffly. "What can they do?"

Then a young man stepped forward from a group. Diffidently, he introduced himself: "I am Paco Escobar, Señor Martinez."

Arturo scrutinised Paco's face. "Your name sounds familiar." His wife Carmen held his arm. Then he clutched his chest. "*Madre de Dios*, it was you who—"

"Señor Martinez," Paco interrupted, "I am sorry to cause you so much anguish." He half-turned, gestured at the fields where new almond trees were being planted.

"Money cannot replace what you have lost. But I offer you these young trees as a public act of contrition." He glanced back at Arturo, concern in his eyes. "Will you accept, sir?"

His eyes turned to Carmen first, and she briefly nodded, then Arturo looked at Paco. "Thank you. I would like to accept, but I am too old to nurture these new trees."

Paco flushed. He didn't seem to know what to say next.

Then someone pushed through the group watching this interchange. "I will accept for my father," said Rafael. He was in his shirtsleeves, covered in dust and ash. "I will bring this orchard back to bloom."

Arturo straightened. "Then, I am content." He shrugged off Carmen's arm. "I can manage." He studied her for a moment. "It's about time you had a new washing machine." And before she could argue, he added, "Though if the drought continues, I don't know if we'll have any water to put in it."

Carmen laughed until tears ran down her cheeks.

"And Rafael?"

"Yes, Father?"
Arturo's eyes sparkled. "Don't forget the orchard needs bees."

Leon Cazador, P.I.

SHATTERED DREAM

I'd seen it coming, of course, but there wasn't much I could do about it, even though I do help the local and national police from time to time. As an interested observer—my brother lived nearby—I introduced myself while Bernard Jackson lifted open the bar café's metal shutters: "*Buenos días*, Señor Jackson, my name is Leon Cazador, and I just called by to wish you well in your new enterprise."

"What're you after?" he wanted to know. He moved over to a stack of red plastic tables and started separating them, lining them up on the patio. He wiped warehouse dust off the surface of one and scowled. "You selling something?"

"No, Señor, I am only concerned that you might not be aware of the niceties of the community spirit out here in Spain."

He swore and added, "Get lost!" Turning his back on me, he fumed, "Damned Spaniards!" He stormed into the dark confines of his newly furnished bar. "Think they own the country!"

I didn't get the chance to explain that I was only half-Spanish.

Jackson wasn't very bright, otherwise he wouldn't have bought the lease to the bar in the first place. Obviously, he hadn't done the necessary homework. The bar was situated in a commercial centre in the middle of a residential area so common sense said that he was going to be unpopular with the neighbours if he resorted to loud live music. And, worse still, he hadn't bothered to get the bar soundproofed or even obtained the appropriate licenses.

Apparently, the first evening wasn't so bad, a reasonable rendering of songs from the Sixties, but my brother Juan, a *Guardia Civil* officer, heard the sound two blocks away.

The second evening was abysmal, as they'd opted for Karaoke. I can't sing and wouldn't wish to inflict my voice on anybody. Yet, thanks to the Japanese, who have a penchant for thinking up torture-like game shows and invented Karaoke—is there a connection?—Juan had to suffer that, too.

But he was slow in complaining. Another neighbour, Victor Welldrew, much closer to the bar, had called in the local police and raised a *denuncia*.

The police stopped the music and were obliged to tell Jackson who had complained.

Light touch-paper and retire.

Jackson's wife stamped round to Welldrew's villa and hammered on the aluminum paneled gates until Victor came out. Then she let fly with a torrent of abuse. There's a Spanish term for her. Roughly translated, it says, *She should have her mouth washed out with salt.* The reasoning goes that salt is for curing meat and maybe it will cure her tongue. Sounds like wishful thinking to me, though.

As far as Jackson was concerned, we Spanish had our noisy fiestas that went on into the early hours of the morning, so why couldn't he have his live music to pull in the tourists' cash? He was deaf to the argument that his noise was persistent every week while fiestas were quite infrequent.

For months it went on, and Welldrew resorted to going to bed with a sleeping pill and earplugs on Friday and Saturday nights. He was too proud to ask anyone to do anything about the noise.

For a stranger in a strange land, Jackson was surprisingly arrogant. "I have a livelihood to think of here, damn you!" he snarled at Victor one day. "Seems to me you've all come here to die. You want to get a life!"

To hell with the neighbours seemed to be his credo. So he shouldn't have been surprised that his neighbours were possibly too busy stoking fires below to frequent his bar for lunchtime meals and a drink.

Playing the devil's advocate, I paid a visit twice and the food was passable English fare. I had some sympathy for Jackson and others like him. It seems a shame that dreams—of avarice?—might collapse. People should strive to realise their dreams, so long as they don't blatantly infringe on the rights of others.

Jackson tried a variety of methods to pull in the public. 'Punters,' he called them, which even to my half-English ear sounded a little derogatory. Magic shows, salsa nights, Sixties revivals and even pornographic TV channels, all with not particularly loud recorded music.

Sadly, he was unaware that he needed an attitude bypass operation if his venture was going to succeed.

Money was being poured in for entertainment but he didn't get enough 'punters' to cover the costs.

Unhappily, illegal drugs are present in every country. One of my informers told me that Jackson stumbled on a couple of young lads indulging themselves in their life-shortening habit, and once the dealer got wind of Jackson's precarious financial situation, he hooked the man well and good. In return for using the bar as an outlet for the merchandise, Jackson would be recompensed with hard cash. Considering his parlous financial affairs, it was too tempting.

Anyone with common sense knows that drugs ruin lives, destroy families, feed crime and of course kill, slowly or prematurely. Drug peddlers are adept at finding someone's weakness and mining it. Because they know that once you're hooked, you're no longer your own person. You belong to the peddler. Revoke all individuality, all self-worth.

Jackson wasn't stupid enough to try the stuff himself. He probably reasoned that as drugs got sold anyway, he might as well profit from the action, right?

Some people in these modern times of instant gratification can't say *no*.

And when things go wrong, it's always somebody else's fault.

It takes quite a while to amass sufficient evidence that will stand up in our courts, so I was biding my time. Eventually, though, I was all set to arrange a National Police drugs raid when the local police finally got tired with all the complaints leveled against Jackson. The police were fed up, then. Ironic, I suppose, to be fed up with a place that serves food. A notice was issued to close down his bar, effective tomorrow. But I wasn't the only one to learn about this constraint.

That rather hot evening I reluctantly knocked on the café bar door and saw his vague silhouette behind the obscure glass partition.

Jackson fiddled with the locks and opened the door slightly. There were no lights on inside: probably saving electricity, or more likely he'd been cut off.

Nobody else was about, he'd had to let his staff go. His wife, threatening divorce, had flown back to mother in England two days earlier.

"What do you want?" Surly as ever. His eyes showed he was lacking sleep, much like his neighbours had done for several months before. And he'd lost some weight around the gut: every cloud, as they say in England, a place indeed beset with clouds.

"I came to warn you that your dealer friends are displeased. Through your persistent stubbornness you've managed to get your bar closed down," I explained. "My contacts tell me that they were making a nice profit here."

"Contacts? What're you talking about?"

"The National Police are about to get interested in you, too," I went on. "Generally, these dealers get violent and vengeful when they're displeased. Do I make myself clear?"

He paled. "What's it to you, anyway?"

"I'd rather you were arrested before your turning a blind eye causes more misery, but I don't particularly want to see you dead. Though I can't vouch for your much-aggrieved neighbours."

He was having difficulty containing his anger. His hands balled into fists at his side. "Who *are* you?"

"I'm the well-wisher you turned away. I suggest you take my advice and leave the country quickly, like now, Señor Jackson. I know for a fact that the dealers are sending two clean-up men round tonight, while the police won't call until tomorrow morning."

His eyes darted over my shoulder, down the street. "Clean-up men? What do I want with cleaners?"

"They tidy up loose ends. Quite efficiently, I hear."

He gulped, the penny finally dropped. "And I'm a loose end?"

"From their point of view, yes."

He swore and shut the door in my face.

If the arrogant unpleasant man didn't heed my warning, it would be his funeral, as the saying goes.

Leon Cazador, P.I.

OFF PLAN

I was wearing a false moustache, gray coloured contact lenses, and my hair was dyed black. My brother, Juan, wouldn't recognise me. In fact, I had difficulty recognising me. I was no longer Leon Cazador but Carlos Ortiz Santos. Sometimes it was necessary to wear a disguise and take on a fake name to hoodwink the ungodly. This was one of those times.

"If you can't come up with the €75,000, Alonso," I said, "then I will make the offer to the other two developers." I tapped the regional map impatiently with a forefinger. "The mayor wants the money soon, so it can all be settled."

Alonso Vargas was slim and appeared urbane in his smart suit. He was convincing in his tone and words. The perfect conman, it seemed. "It is difficult, Carlos. That is a great deal of money." He was toying with me, playing for time, and debating whether I would bargain. His dark eyes glinted. I knew it wasn't with humor but greed. He rubbed his pointed chin, pretending to think. He needed a kick.

I sighed resignedly and started folding up the map.

"No, no, Carlos," he said and urgently gripped my forearm and halted my retiring action. "I have the money, as promised." He eyed the *Mercadona* supermarket bag at his feet.

"That's good, Alonso." I smiled and left the map half-folded.

He cocked his head to one side. "I suppose it would be foolish of me to ask for a receipt?"

I grinned and nodded. "That would be foolish, yes. The mayor has to pay several anxious people to adjust various documents. Others, they need financial incentives to keep their mouths shut." I shrugged. "You know how it is."

"Ah, yes." His eyes glimmered with the prospect of four hundred acres of re-designated land, all his to build upon. "I know how it is." His foot gently moved the plastic bag over the tiled floor towards me.

Leaning down and picking it up, I asked, "So, you can bring me the final installment next week, as agreed?"

"Cash flow is difficult, times are not so good since the building boom has slowed down, you know." He shrugged pronounced shoulders. "The crisis, it bites deeply."

Shaking my head, I quickly finished folding the map. "If you cannot honour our agreement, then I must go elsewhere. We agreed you would pay me two instalments." I slid the bag across the table, in plain view.

Anxiety was written all over his face. He glanced left and right, but nobody seemed to be paying us any attention.

"I'm not one of your clients, Alonso. Delay is not an option."

"No, no," he said hastily, pushing the bag towards me. "Please, take this now. It is difficult, but not impossible. I will have the rest of the money."

"You're sure?"

He nodded and offered the same smooth trusting smile he turned on for his clients. "You have my word," he said.

I stood up. "Your word is good enough for me, Alonso," I lied and shook his offered hand. I turned and left the bar with the bag of money under my arm.

**

Doris and Frank Chambers were in their sixties. Serious Hispanophiles. They loved the land, the culture, the history and particularly the Spanish people. Well, most of them. Alonso Vargas didn't fall into that blessed category. Sadly, in his case they'd been too trusting.

I'm ashamed of some of my countrymen, the way they treat the *extranjeros* who plough vast sums of money into our country. It's a bit difficult for me, being half-English. On the other side of the coin, I'm also ashamed of those many English countrymen of mine who lack manners or understanding and want to Anglo-form what they see as their little part of Spain.

Alonso Vargas was just one of many plying his crooked trade in the Costa Blanca area. It must have been like this in those gold rush places, whether they were the gold fields of the Klondike, California and Australia, or the diamond mines of South Africa. Wherever there's money to be had and dreams to be fulfilled, clinging to the new towns or urbanizations you'll find the ungodly, greedily duping the weak and the unknowing. This part of Spain is no different, save that instead of gold or diamonds, it's usually land and property.

Off plan properties are generally safe buys these days, providing you deal with a reputable firm. Sadly, many visitors from Britain or Finland, Iceland or Belgium, don't do their homework. A sorry few seem to leave their brains in their home country. Others are victims of complex scams or smooth-talking conmen.

Alonso fell into the latter category. He was one of six similar operators I'd been interested in for about three months. Ever since Mr. Chambers was arrested, in fact.

The Chambers couple was distraught and virtually destitute. Juan, my brother in the *Guardia Civil*, told me their sad story. They'd saved for a dream villa but illness and the British government ruined most of their plans so they ended up compromising, sinking all they had left—€89,000—into an off plan property Alonso had earmarked for them.

Naturally, Alonso assured them that the country *finca* would command a gorgeous view of the mountains. Because the dwelling was inland, it was reasonably priced, he said. Mrs. Chambers would have preferred to be nearer to a town, especially as her arthritis was troublesome, but the finca was all they could afford. Besides, Frank argued, the climate would probably ease her pains anyway. They decided to take out a small mortgage to cover the difference between their initial payment and the full cost of the house.

Of course, Alonso didn't use his real name. When dealing with Mr. and Mrs. Chambers, he was Jacinto Diaz Rodriguez of *Salteador SA*. He was quite cheeky, using that company name, considering it meant 'robber' or 'highwayman' as most of his transactions were in effect highway robbery. Alonso had at least four other aliases and as many fake companies.

When Frank Chambers applied to the bank for a mortgage, he had neglected to get the full details from Alonso. Anxious to finalise the paperwork, Frank went round to the Salteador office. But Frank's heart sank when he noticed that the office was boarded up. In his stumbling Spanish, he enquired in the neighbouring premises. It seemed that Jacinto—Alonso—had only been there for six months. Frank did the logical thing and went to the police and to the British consul, but there was little they could do to recover the money or locate Alonso.

Stress seemed to aggravate Doris's arthritis. Their funds were quickly depleted as they paid for translators and forked out for their monthly townhouse rent. Finally, Frank had a brainwave and forced his way into the abandoned office in search of clues. The place was deserted, all the furniture had gone. Even the electrical fittings had been taken. A few Telefonica and Iberdrola bills lay on the tiled floor and that was all. He sank down on the floor then, a broken man.

The *policia local* found Frank there and arrested him for breaking and entering. That's when my brother Juan heard about the case and took an interest.

***

"This is for you both." I put the *Mercadona* bag on the coffee table in front of us. We were in their cramped townhouse lounge. The pine furniture had seen better days and was decidedly careworn. Dressed in a smart flower-patterned dress, her hair in need of a perm, Doris sat nursing a mug of soup—that and *menus del día* at the nearby Chinese restaurant were all they could now afford.

Frank opened the bag and let out a gasp. "My God, look at this, Doris! There must be thousands of euros!" His eyes lit up in wonderment.

Doris lowered her mug to the table, her rheumy eyes moving from her husband to me. "Mr. Cazador?"

"It's a refund from the Salteador firm," I said, which was truthful enough.

Taking the notes out, Frank riffled through the piles, trying to count them.

"I think you'll find it's correct," I said. "€89,000."

Doris beamed and the creases of age diminished. "Gosh, they haven't even kept the deposit," she said.

"That's damned decent of them, Mr. Cazador," said Frank.

"Next time I see Jacinto Rodriguez, I'll be sure to tell him you said that." I didn't linger to accept their thanks but did manage to get them both to promise to be more circumspect in their dealings with property developers. I left the names of a couple of firms I could vouch for who'd give them a fair deal.

***

Leon Cazador, P.I.

When I returned to meet Alonso for the second installment, the National Police accompanied me and I wasn't wearing the disguise of Carlos Ortiz Santos. I had presented adequate evidence and affidavits together with my denunciation, carefully excluding any mention of the hapless Chambers couple.

"I swear the Santos swine is to blame!" Alonso shouted as the cuffs were snapped on his wrists.

The arresting policeman laughed. "We've heard of this Santos guy before! He doesn't exist. He's a figment of your imagination."

Detective Chaparieta added, "You're not the first villain to use him as an excuse, either!"

The arresting officer reeled off Alonso's aliases, including Jacinto Rodriguez, as he made his charge.

Alonso growled, "What about this money I've brought? Won't it tempt you to let me go?"

"No," said the policeman sternly. His swarthy face appeared like thunder. "You insult me and my uniform to even suggest a bribe."

"It will be used as evidence," the detective explained. "Perhaps the courts will allocate it to some of your unfortunate victims, no?"

The dark look on Alonso's face was little repayment for the anguish, heartache and sheer hell he'd put so many trusting souls through. But I thought that it would do for now.

Plenty more ungodly were languishing in the mistaken belief that they'd get away with their ill-gotten gains. My name translated into English was 'Lion Hunter'. The Spanish sounded less pretentious. Julio Iglesias probably would agree that his name doesn't sound so fine in English as July Church, no relation to Charlotte, of course. I left them to it, determined to continue my crusade to hunt down those despicable people, from whatever country, who had no conscience.

Nik Morton

Leon Cazador, P.I.

DRAGON LADY

Nǐ hǎo, Meizhen," I said—*hello* in Mandarin—as I walked into Meizhen Teng's private hospital room. "Fancy meeting you here." I spoke in English, as my 'common speech', Putonghua or Mandarin, was admittedly a bit rusty. There are plenty of Chinese restaurants and bazaars here on the Costa Blanca, but the opportunity to use the language is still limited.

"Carlos Santos?" Meizhen said and struggled to sit up, which must have been difficult as both her legs were covered in plaster and in traction. This was a shame as I recalled that she had rather attractive legs. "It is good to see you, after how many years?"

"Nine," I said. I'd been undercover in Beijing at the time, which explained her use of my alias.

Meizhen had been one of many brave souls working against her government's continual repression in an organisation called Free All Chinese from Oppression (FACO).

She'd proven to be a born leader and everyone thought she was very dependable and managed to get things done. She deprecated, saying that she was just plodding and methodical. That way, though, she never lost sight of her goal.

I wondered what had happened to make her leave her homeland. At least she didn't appear to be scarred by her exile here in Spain, though she was certainly bruised and battered at the moment.

"I'm surprised you remembered me," she said, an amused glint in her dark eyes. "I thought all Chinese look the same to Westerners."

"How could I forget you? You haven't aged a bit!"

"*Xiéxie*." *Thank you.*

"Besides," I added, "your name's on the door."

She grinned and I'm sure would have thrown something at me but fortunately there were no appropriate missiles at hand on the bedside cupboard.

She winced as the bubbling laughter started to move other muscles.

I leaned over and gave her a light kiss on her cool, smooth, round cheek. I glimpsed a sepia tattoo poking through her jacket collar; I recalled she had exotic patterns on her back and some intimate places.

Then I sat on the chair by the bed. "How did you manage to fall off a fourth apartment balcony and survive?"

Her eyes shone in the light and her thin lips curved, but she wasn't smiling. "Just an accident. Silly, really." In fact, I'd been told that a truckload of wooden pallets had broken her fall and her legs.

It was obvious that Meizhen was being evasive. Fortunately, she didn't worry too much about losing face so I could continue to question her directly: "You're not still working for FACO, are you?"

"No." She shook her head. "I managed to get out. Now, I'm in the restaurant business."

My turn to grin. And I was surprised to feel relief flood over me. It was just a coincidence, then, that one of Kwan's many apartments was in the same block as that from which Meizhen launched her death-defying dive. "Not *another* Chinese restaurant?" I laughed. "We've got them coming out of our ears!"

"This one is special," she said with a hint of pride in her voice. "I half-own *The Dragon Lady*."

My heart sank and my eyes must have showed concern since she glanced away. Someone once said there are no such things as coincidences. "What is your relationship with Ho Kwan?" I asked.

Meizhen's face turned serious, but her eyes tended to evade mine. "Why all these questions? It is not like you."

She smoothed the sheet at her left side, patted it. "Well, you were always inquisitive in Beijing, I know, but when we got to know each other better, you showed a more tender side."

Our eyes met, lingered.

They were good memories. I sighed, shaking them off.

She hadn't answered my question. "I'm going out on a limb here by telling you this," I said.

"And you still work for..?"

"Myself, mostly."

She grinned, almost her old self again, but there was a wariness in her now. "Mostly. A most unhelpful answer." She nodded her head. "Inscrutable. Almost Chinese."

"You honour me, Meizhen." I gave her a mock bow. "Actually, we're staking out *The Dragon Lady*," I said. "A raid is imminent."

Ho Kwan was a Snake and proud of it. According to Chinese astrology, his year of birth, 1965, was the year of the Snake, which meant that he would be lucky with money. Many Chinese were superstitious and great gamblers, and Ho Kwan was both.

Even though Chinese restaurants proliferate at an almost exponential scale in Spain, there always seemed room for one more. The Chinese were not afraid of hard work and long hours, and in five years, Ho Kwan had built up *The Dragon Lady* into one of the best in the area.

Kwan came to Spain in 1999, worked diligently and expected the same from his fellow associates. A man of keen intelligence, he tended to trust nobody but himself.

A few associates suggested, in whispers, that Kwan's lack of humility was as a result of a retiring nature and an overriding confidence in his abilities, which were considerable. He had come to the notice of the security service two years ago and a rather bulging dossier had been compiled since.

Many hard-working Chinese had to pay Kwan protection money. Others were virtually in servitude to his organisation, merely working to eat and glean some shelter over their heads. If some enterprise was criminal, then it seemed that Kwan had a slice of the action.

"Ho doesn't have the slightest idea anyone is onto him," Meizhen said. "If I'd known, I wouldn't have gone near him. Honestly, I wouldn't want to upset your plans." She gave me an earnest look.

"I believe you, Meizhen. Actually, I've called in a favour for you."

"Oh?" Her forehead wrinkled slightly and an impeccable eyebrow rose. "Why do I need help?"

"A search among the pallets on the truck turned up the silenced pistol you must have dropped when you landed. Fully loaded with 7.62mm Type 64 rimless cartridges. Made in China."

Her eyes widened, daring me to go on.

"I suggested the weapon should simply be impounded as dangerous, source unknown."

"*Xiéxie*." She bowed her head briefly. "I am in your debt."

I leaned closer. "Do you mean that?"

She nodded.

"Then tell me why you wanted to kill Ho Kwan."

She glanced at the closed door, then at the overhead lighting and wall-mounted television.

"This hospital may be state-of-the-art," I said, "but it isn't bugged."

After a moment, she pursed her lips and nodded. "I believe you, Carlos."

"Call me Leon," I said. "It's about time. Leon Cazador."

Meizhen shrugged, dismissing the deception of my alias. "We all have to wear masks, don't we? Sometimes it is simply to save face, and at other times it is to save our lives."

"Just so." I smiled.

She eased back on her pillow and her lips curved. "I suppose I should explain."

When Meizhen was a teenage student, she was in love with an older student called Wang Lee. This was in 1989 and the time of the student unrest and so-called rebellion in Tiananmen Square in Beijing. The government sent in the troops and on 4 June, there was a massacre of the innocents.

"Just like those brave people in Czechoslovakia in 1968 when the Russians invaded," Meizhen said, her eyes moist at the memory. "We wanted to demonstrate peacefully. But they crushed us. Wang was nineteen and he stood in front of a row of tanks, stubbornly not moving."

She shivered at the memory. "I screamed for him to come off the road, but he just turned to me and smiled and stood his ground, daring the tanks to move against him. He was there for about thirty minutes. I had just rallied some friends to rush out to drag him to safety when a government snatch squad grabbed Wang." Now the tears flowed freely. "He glanced back at me and looked fearful, more scared of the soldiers than he had been of the tanks."

"I think I remember seeing the photo. That was him, was it?"

Meizhen nodded. "I never heard from Wang again. Rumours spread in the aftermath. That he was executed, that he was sent to a rehabilitation farm..."

"I don't see what all this has to do with Ho Kwan."

"The leader of the snatch squad was Ho Kwan," Meizhen said. "I saw him very clearly, and I will never forget him."

For seventeen years, she had stubbornly tracked down Kwan. Perhaps I will never know what happened in the apartment. She wasn't willing to tell me more. The Chinese automatic pistol with integral silencer had a magazine capacity of nine rounds. It was found with seven cartridges loaded. Maybe she got off two shots at Kwan's bodyguards? If she'd been attempting his assassination, then she'd failed, since Kwan had obviously survived.

Her bruises could have been as a result of a beating as much as being sustained from landing on those pallets. Did she jump to evade more punishment or was she pushed?

***

The raid on *The Dragon Lady* went well. The *Guardia Civil*, the National Police and local police came away with tons of drugs, wads of money in a number of currencies, several laptops, assorted automatic weapons and other electronic equipment. They also sequestered two cars and three vans, all found to contain traces of drugs.

Ho Kwan and six confederates were arrested.

The raid received ten lines of newsprint coverage and a Ministry of the Interior photo of certain items in the haul. Most of the details went unreported. After all, it wouldn't do to unduly upset the Chinese as Spain was angling for favourable trading deals with their government.

About two months after the raid, Meizhen was able to walk with the aid of sticks. She was as stubborn as an ox and pushed herself as well as anybody else in order to get what she wanted. I suppose I might have come into that category, too.

Displaying smart business acumen, she bought *The Dragon Lady* restaurant outright and managed to get me to keep her up-to-date on the trial of Ho Kwan. His entire organisation was now in tatters, which pleased all of us.

But our pleasure was short-lived. While Ho Kwan was transported to a judicial hearing, the prison wagon was in an accident at a crossroads. Nobody was seriously hurt, but Kwan was freed. He escaped on the back of a motorcycle. After that, a number of us started looking over our shoulders.

***

Yet another sunny day reminded me that there was not a lot to miss in the UK. The sun beamed down on the boardwalk veranda of *The Dragon Lady* restaurant. Meizhen sat opposite me and poured my red wine then replenished her glass of *agua sin gas*. "Business is booming, Leon."

"I'm glad to hear it." More by habit than necessity, I glanced over my shoulder, but we were unobserved.

"The news on the grapevine has reached me," she said.

I nodded and manipulated the chopsticks to pick up another succulent piece from my dish of *yǎrou fán*—duck with white rice.

She said, her tone matter-of-fact, "Ho Kwan's body was washed up on the rocks in Alicante Bay yesterday."

"I'd heard but didn't bother getting in touch. I guessed you'd have contacts to inform you."

"Yes, I have many contacts, Leon. You know, I'm an Ox."

"I'm aware of your birth date," I said.

"Of course, you would be, wouldn't you? I suppose you know everything about me."

"Not everything." I thought about her fall from that apartment block. I reached out, took her small hand.

"Some things are best kept secret from friends, Leon."

"Perhaps you're right." She was most perceptive. I didn't want my suspicions confirmed. I had no desire to know that Meizhen's many contacts had engineered Ho Kwan's breakout. I certainly didn't want to know that she was present when Kwan was executed and cast into the sea.

I let go of her hand and resumed eating, though the food seemed to have lost its flavour.

"Ho Kwan was a Snake," she said.

"In more ways than one," I suggested.

She smiled. "It's ironic, really, but according to the Chinese Zodiac, we were supposed to be a most compatible match—Ox and Snake."

Leon Cazador, P.I.

I sipped the rich fruity wine. It tasted just fine. "Well, I think he met his match with you," I said.

Nik Morton

Leon Cazador, P.I.

CRY WOLF

Fernando Lopez was what you would call, in English, a poacher turned gamekeeper. A cunning rather than a clever man, he had been a hunter of wolves—a *lobero*—for many years, learning the tracking skills from his father and his father before him.

When I was fifteen, our parents brought us to stay in Spain for almost a year. "Family problems," Mother said. And during that time, my brother Juan and I often left Pilar behind and went into the mountains to track wild animals and bring home a brace of rabbits. During one of these escapades, we stumbled upon forty-year-old Fernando who was setting a trap to catch a lone wolf. That was thirty years ago. Wolf traps are now illegal.

Fernando was taciturn but somehow we three got along. Perhaps our youthful enthusiasm and respect for his lore was appreciated. Anyway, he asked us to join him on a wolf hunt the following week. Although we knew we would have to concoct some innocuous story for our mother to cover our absence, we couldn't miss this opportunity, so we agreed. Our friendship grew from that time on.

Thirty years ago, the wolf was regarded as a pest. "The wolf must be exterminated as its continued existence is a blemish on our standing in the civilised world," the mayor of Fernando's town had declared. "Spain appears to be a Third World country. We must get rid of the wolf plagues, as Britain and France have done, so we can be civilised."

The government of the day offered bounties for dead wolves and even supplied strychnine to landowners and the peasants who worked the land. It would be interesting to find out whether the incidence of new widows and widowers increased from this period.

Fernando didn't hold with such cowardly measures. "I've seen their gruesome deaths. They say it is quick, but by God, it is painful also. Pests are still God's creatures, no?"

He respected the wolf but believed his job was necessary and relished the hunt, pitting his wits against the ancient carnivore.

I learned a great deal from Fernando, and not only about tracking, but then our family had to return to England. Still, we'd kept in touch and as the years passed, Fernando didn't envy my traveling the globe. He was comfortable in his world of nature right here in Spain.

Fernando's transformation happened a few years before the European wolf was considered an endangered species. After working in intelligence and law enforcement around the world, I'd briefly returned to Spain and was involved in a clandestine operation against a couple of London gang bosses, in the days when extradition wasn't so easy. When that job was over, I decided to look up Fernando.

"Leon, *amigo*, the years have been kind to you!" he exclaimed. His left leg was in a plaster cast from ankle to crotch. He struggled to stand.

"Don't get up," I said, and hurried forward to shake his hand and give him a hug. "What happened to you?"

"Ha, it was my own stupid fault," he said, tapping his left ear. "I'm going deaf as well as daft. I was out tracking a pack of wolves, when a wild boar attacked me from behind." He swore colourfully. "*Madre de Dios*, he gored me. The infernal beast wouldn't leave me alone. It was as if it had a taste of me and liked it."

"That's terrible, old friend. You were lucky, I guess."

"The animal was possessed, Leon!" he said. "I've seen the wanton destruction of *lobadas,* but never thought I'd be the object of it—especially from a boar!"

Lobadas are blood-lusting attacks where wolves, like many carnivores including the fox, often get excited by the scent of blood and slaughter so that they kill far more prey than they can possibly eat. I'd heard it said of foxes and it was also true of wolves: "They are their own worst enemy." Yet, it's nature in the raw, tooth and claw, and who are we to judge?

"Then, by God," Fernando went on, "five wolves—I swear it was the ones I was tracking—burst through the undergrowth. I thought I was finished. But they attacked the boar, not me!"

Tears filled this hard man's eyes. "They ignored me and my bloody leg. They went for the boar!" He could hardly sit still, his hands gesticulating. "The pack dragged the boar to its knees and finished it off."

He shook his head, light gray eyes blazing at the memory. "One of the wolves, I suspect it was the leader, glanced over its shoulder at me." He grinned and I wondered about the old tales about *llobadío*, a wicked curse transmitted by the gaze of a wolf.

Fernando wiped his brow. "I stared right back at him and he turned away. Then they pulled their kill into the undergrowth and I was left alone."

"What did you do?"

"My artery hadn't been cut, fortunately," he said. "I used my shirt to bandage the wound and staggered, well, limped, with a branch as a stick, to the road." He shrugged. "A man in a passing van picked me up, took me to hospital. I was in shock. Nobody believed me. *I* hardly believed me!"

From that day on, Fernando never hunted wolves.

Now, all these years later, I was again visiting him and his wife, Lucita. Their home and the surrounding garden appeared in exceptionally good condition, considering both of them were in their seventies.

"My wolves are becoming the scapegoat," he said over a dinner prepared by Lucita—*conejo a la cazadora*— cooked in my honour, she had said. It certainly excited my taste-buds and brought back memories of adolescence.

"Your wolves?" I queried.

"Yes, I protect them now. I am a conservationist." He grimaced. "It is hard. Many of the local people, they are still filled with superstition."

I nodded, understanding. Even these days, many villagers won't mention a wolf by name but rather use an innocuous expression such as *amigo* and *el otro*, as they fear that by speaking the word "*lobo*" they invoke its evil spirit.

Fear of wolves is engrained. The cave paintings in Los Arcos in Jaén depict its infernal bestial character. As far back as pre-Roman Spain, the wolf was strongly linked with the afterlife as these animals often gorged on human corpses, treating them as carrion. Then, of course, the *hombre-lobo*—the werewolf—was invented in the Middle Ages and the animal's fate seemed sealed for extinction; the wolves literally hounded to death, at the cost of many hounds, no doubt.

"We must do something before it is too late for my wolves, Leon," Fernando said.

***

Next morning, dawn light crested the mountains and the air shimmered, as if awakening. Fernando and I set out with our rifles over our shoulders. This was a different kind of hunt, though. I also carried a digital camera.

Within an hour, we were on the trail of Fernando's wolves. Despite his age and the serious damage inflicted by the boar, he moved stealthily, like a shadow beside me. So many wolf hunts end in failure, because the animals are exceedingly elusive. But even when he hunted to kill them, Fernando seemed to have an affinity with *el lobo*.

Concealed behind a craggy rock that overlooked a mountainside meadow, we watched the five wolves in their lair. Each one had the distinctive black marks along the tail, back, jowls and front legs. Their coats glistened healthily. They were eating the carcass of a wild dog.

Earlier, I'd telephoned a friend in the *Oficina de Estadísticas* and he told me that an estimated ninety thousand dogs were abandoned in Spain last year. It didn't take a statistician to conclude that the outcast big dogs wouldn't hesitate to tackle sheep. They had to eat, after all.

Señor Ruben Rivera, Fernando's neighbour, was a sheep farmer and blamed the loss of his sheep—a not insubstantial ten per week—on the wolves. He was about to muster a hunting party "to be rid of the wolves for good".

Fernando argued that it was probably wild dogs to blame, but Rivera wouldn't listen.

Farmers were awarded compensation for wolf attacks, though it had been known that some sheep farmers had put in compensation claims for more sheep than actually existed in the province. And, apparently, certain Partido Popular councillors once even encouraged farmers to register vastly inflated death statistics for their own ends. Sadly, the wolf was no match for party politics and greed.

Soundlessly, the pair of us both moved away from our vantage point and headed across country onto Rivera's land. Eventually we crested a rocky knoll and, ahead and below, a flock of sheep grazed, quite contented.

We didn't have to wait long.

Two sleek shapes darted in among the outlying sheep and downed one each. I aimed my rifle and fired.

The animal yelped as my shot pierced its flank. Its companion growled and sniffed the air. Fernando fired and the second intruder fell across the bleating sheep.

Loping over the rugged terrain, we hurried up to our targets while the rest of the flock continued to graze, unconcerned.

I took several photographs and then used my mobile phone.

About an hour later, the *policia local* officer arrived with Señor Rivera.

"What is the meaning of this?" Rivera demanded. He was stocky, beetle-browed and missing several teeth. "You're on my property." Then he saw the sheep. "*Madre de Dios*! More victims of those wolves!"

"I don't think so, neighbour," said Fernando. He pointed at the two drugged dogs.

I knelt down beside them and removed the darts. "They'll be unconscious for a while yet," I explained.

"These are your so-called wolves, Señor," Fernando said. "I brought along Señor Cazador as a witness."

Rivera gaped and the policeman took off his hat and scratched his head.

"They're not even feral dogs," I said, fingering their collars. "These are the bull mastiffs of Señor Nogales, your other neighbour. He puts them out at night, and, clearly, they attack your livestock. And during the day they spend their time sleeping under the kitchen table, doubtless dreaming of their next hunt."

"Nogales, eh?" said Rivera, grinding the few teeth he had left.

I stood and added, "Perhaps if Señor Nogales fed his dogs at home, they would leave your sheep alone."

Rivera scowled and nodded. Then he turned to the police officer. "We need to see Señor Nogales, straight away!" The pair of them tramped off the way they'd come and Fernando stood, arms akimbo, chuckling.

After that, all talk of hunting wolves was dropped. Some time later, on one moonlit evening, Fernando took me out into the hills and we watched two wolf cubs playing beside their mother. The she-wolf scented us but didn't display alarm. "She knows," Fernando whispered, tapping the side of his nose. "I will protect them, my wolves."

I envied him. They were indeed Fernando's wolves.

Leon Cazador, P.I.

ENDANGERED SPECIES

He had large eyes, big ears and, surprisingly, his middle finger was very long on each hand.

"He looks cute," I said, lowering the photograph of the little aye-aye. His hair was black, and he had a long bushy tail. His eyes seemed to be expressing surprise at finding himself in a cage rather than the diminishing rainforests of Madagascar. Perhaps the daylight conditions affected him, too, which wasn't strange really, as his kind is nocturnal. "But," I added, shaking my head in mock concern, "my fiancée wants something a bit more exotic. Know what I mean?"

"A pity, Señor Santos, because we have many aye-ayes." Lazaro Perez shrugged his broad shoulders as if the fate of his primates was of little concern to him.

It was a hot day, as usual, and we were glad of the air-conditioning in the roadside bar. Condensation formed little globules on the sides of our small glasses of *Mahou* beer. The plates had recently contained tasty *tapas* but were now empty, save for the odd breadcrumb.

Brushing a few crumbs off the table, Perez slid across another colour photograph. "This, I think, will be more to your fiancée's taste, no?"

In times like these, I wondered what in my childhood had influenced me to lie so well. While I certainly had a lady close to my heart, I had no fiancée. My calling required that I adopted an alias from time to time, and as far as Perez and his business associates were concerned, I was Carlos Ortiz Santos, rather than my true self, Leon Cazador. What was one's true self, though? I shook off such heavy introspective thoughts and studied the photograph.

It showed a large boa constrictor, beautifully marked with cream, brown, tan and gray camouflage ovals and diamonds.

"That's more like it!" I said enthusiastically. I'd played enough poker games to know that my face betrayed none of my true emotions.

Such exquisite skin belonged on the reptile, not on somebody's feet or handbag. Still, I was being marginally unkind to Señor Perez whose business was finding expensive homes for exotic pets and not slaughtering endangered species for eye-catching fashion accessories.

"Impressive, isn't he?"

"Yes," I agreed. "How big is he?"

Grinning, Perez produced a handful of photographs. "We have three males and one female. They range from two to five metres in length." He added with a note of pride, "The female is pregnant, which is good news for our business."

"Your suppliers are good," I said, flicking the photograph to discourage a wine-fly. "These animals are hard to find nowadays."

"Much of their habitat is being destroyed," Perez said. "We do them a service, preserving them in the hands of discerning private individuals like you, Señor."

"Yes, I can see that. My fiancée has always wanted to do exotic dancing. But I think the big boa might be too heavy for her."

"Yes." He smirked, perhaps picturing a scantily clad woman draped with a big snake. "The small one still weighs fifteen kilos. A lot to hold and dance with."

I pretended to study the two photographs, turning them over to look at the respective cost in euros scrawled on the back. "It's difficult." I bit my lip and stroked my false moustache. "Can I see them first?"

Perez smiled. "You certainly can, Señor. But to show good faith, I would ask that you pay a few thousand on deposit. We have overheads, as you will understand."

"Yes," I said, "no problem."

***

Wearing a blindfold, I was jostled in the back as Perez drove the Toyota Land Cruiser over rough country tracks. Finally, after what I later discovered was two hours, the strip of black cloth was removed. Thankfully, my moustache stayed firmly attached.

Sitting beside me in the back was a cadaverous man who Perez referred to simply as Vadim. Now, as he tucked my blindfold in the pocket of his dungarees, Vadim gave me the benefit of his penetrating stare. With his slicked-back black hair and leaden features, he might well have escaped from a Bela Lugosi film.

The rest of the journey, another hour's duration, took us into the mountains. I didn't recognise any landmarks and hadn't expected to, really.

We rounded a final bend then approached a large fenced-off property in a hollow between two hills. The road was dusty but well used. We drove between the entrance pillars and the gate slid back automatically after us.

The single-storey buildings looked prefab and formed a u-shape. The Land Cruiser braked at the end of the right-hand upright of the 'u' and Vadim said, "Time to get out, sir."

I clambered out, tripped and sank to one knee on the hard compacted dirt. I grabbed the side of the doorframe for support and heaved myself up, massaging my right foot.

"Are you all right, Señor?" Vadim asked.

"Yes, fine, just a bit careless. I was so glad to feel firm ground underfoot again, I slipped." Being knocked around in the back for about three hours was no fun, and I was sure I had a few bruises to prove it. As I made a show of dusting down my trousers with my hands, I surveyed the place. No other vehicles were in sight, so there must have been a garage somewhere. Probably over on the right—that's where most of the tyre tracks led.

Vadim walked over to stand next to me. Then Perez joined us, using a linen handkerchief to wipe his sweaty forehead.

I heard cicadas; they seemed everywhere. But I was after somewhat bigger creatures.

Double doors opened at the end of the 'u' and a man and a woman strode towards us, all smiles. She was dressed in a blue open-necked shirt and jeans, while he wore camouflage trousers and a shirt.

I shook the woman's hand.

"This is Doina Marko, our resident zoologist," explained Perez. "She ensures you get the best product your money can buy."

"Señor Santos, pleased to meet you." She smiled with thin lips, toasted brown eyes lighting up. Her accent was good, but there was a hint of Romanian. She had high cheekbones and almond-shaped eyes. An oval face was framed by black hair that reached her shoulders. About thirty, I guessed.

"Our director, Nicholas Basescu," Perez said, as I shook hands with the snowy-haired man in camouflage fatigues.

Basescu had a hooked nose and it twitched as he talked. "You have brought the money?" he asked, veal-coloured lips forming a smile. Businesslike but not rude. His cheeks were pitted from some serious ailment, and his complexion was sallow.

"Yes, of course." I pulled out the envelope and handed it over.

He barely gave it a glance and passed it to Doina. She eagerly ripped it open and counted the notes, the tip of her tongue sticking out between her lips. "All correct," she said.

Sweat soaked my back. This was always the moment I dreaded most. Would they take the money then dispose of me, or would they be greedy enough to want more? Greed usually won.

Clapping a hand on my shoulder, Basescu said, "Let's show you your little snake!" He'd been reasonably subtle about it—with that gesture, he'd checked that I wasn't carrying a weapon under my lightweight jacket. Some undercover agents never carry guns, as their argument goes that they're not all that reliable and give a false sense of security. Others rely on quick wits and superior unarmed combat skills. I wasn't particular. Today, a knife was strapped to my left calf while my right held a holstered Colt. There was no way they'd know that, unless they blatantly searched me and for the time being I was a valuable client and wasn't to be embarrassed.

Perez went back to the Land Cruiser and drove off, his work done, while the rest of us walked towards the buildings on the left-hand side of the 'u'.

I walked alongside Doina. She exuded the pheromones of a sexual predator, and I was almost smitten as she talked. "Governments make laws, but they don't see the global picture," she said. "Endangered species will die out unless more businesses like ours get in on the act."

"I agree," I said. "You're preaching to the converted here, Miss Marko."

"Doina will do. Carlos, isn't it?"

"Yes. Carlos."

We entered the door at the end of the row. "You'll get a good view from the top," she said. "Follow me." She went ahead and climbed a narrow set of metal stairs that led to a swaying walkway. For a brief moment, I admired her tightly clad buttocks as she ascended, then concentrated on following her. Basescu and Vadim climbed after me.

At the top of the stairs, I stepped onto the walkway, which was suspended from ropes anchored to the ceiling's metal-frame joists. Lianas hung from trees that brushed the ceiling and tree-boles poked up through gaps in the glass below us, all in an attempt at conveying an impression of being immersed in the jungle. I was sweating, but it wasn't due to the humidity inside.

As I walked, I looked down through glass at the endangered species. I passed six cages of aye-ayes, two cages of golden lion marmosets and a dozen glass cases of desert tortoises.

Not so long ago a *Guardia Civil* raid had uncovered several rare Mediterranean tortoises smuggled into Spain from Slovenia, each one liable to fetch up to €12,000. That was small beer compared to this lot. I wondered what was in the buildings on the right-hand side.

Finally, we stopped at the end section and Doina's hand held my arm; an electric charge seemed to flash through me. "I think you'll like this exhibit," she whispered.

Behind me, I heard Vadim chuckle.

One of the boas was feeding on a rabbit, stretching its mouth to accommodate the dead animal. "It doesn't have fangs," Doina explained with enthusiasm. "It simply crushes the breath out of its victim."

"I see," I said. "It leaves me quite breathless."

"Nice joke, Señor Santos!" said Basescu in his best buttering-up-the-client tone.

Then Doina gasped and shouted, "Oh my God, she's giving birth!"

True enough, next to the feeding boa was the biggest snake, and she was evacuating wriggling little snakes onto the straw-covered floor. Each baby boa was about sixty centimetres long. The sight made my skin crawl.

Doina gripped the handrail. "There must be fifty of them!"

I wasn't counting, but there were too many for my peace of mind. I glanced away, over my shoulder.

At that moment, Vadim's head jerked up like a pointer getting the scent. "What was that, boss?"

Basescu heard the approaching sound and glanced worriedly at Doina, then me.

I'd been expecting them, since the transmitter in my shoe heel would have pinpointed my position accurately enough. I'd switched it on when I got out the Land Cruiser and slipped. "They're *Guardia Civil* helicopters," I said helpfully.

Vadim swore and lunged at me but I sidestepped on the swaying walkway and grabbed his arm, shoved it up his back and flung him back the way he'd come, straight into Basescu.

As they collided, I snatched my knife from its sheath and sliced at the rope supporting the walkway on my left.

The walkway suddenly tilted. I'd been expecting it and held onto the right-hand rail with my right. The others were caught unawares.

Vadim fumbled in vain for a handhold but slid sideways. He shrieked as he fell the short distance onto the glass ceiling of the boa cage. Fine spider web cracks appeared under him. He seemed reluctant to move, his eyes wide, sweat oozing on his forehead.

Basescu held onto the right-hand rail, his left fumbling in his jacket. As he pulled out an automatic, I'd already pulled out my Colt from its ankle holster and fired. The shot hit Basescu's shoulder and he let go, his face suffused with rage. He dropped the pistol and toppled down onto Vadim. The cracking glass sound got louder.

I hung with my left hand, my right clasping the Colt. I glanced at the end of the walkway. Doina was edging back, anxiety on her face. "The boas, if they fall on them," she shouted.

I realised she was worried about the boas, not the men. She seemed unarmed. I couldn't shoot her, and I had no way of incapacitating her.

"I reckon the snakes can take care of themselves," I said.

She nodded and ran to another set of stairs. She gave me one last glance.

I decided to let her go. She could take her chances with the *guardia* who'd be landing any minute now.

"Save me!" Basescu pleaded.

"Sorry, I can't do that," I said. "You are not an endangered species."

The glass ceiling broke, and the two men fell into the cage with the male boa.

Nik Morton

Leon Cazador, P.I.

BIG NOISE

"You've come to the right person, Mr. Santos!" Darren Atkins said, speaking louder than was necessary in the *tapas* bar that overlooked the Plaza Mayor. "My product is the best on Spain's south coast, take my word for it! I'm the big noise around here!"

Every sentence tended to end with an exclamation. This self-styled important person was big in other respects as well. Even when I use my real name, Leon Cazador, rather than my undercover alias of Carlos Santos, I stand six feet high in my open-toed sandals; yet Atkins was a couple of inches taller than me. His Hawaiian-style short-sleeved shirt bulged due to his big muscles and shoulders. Because he had shaved his head, his big ears appeared more prominent and tended to press forward like little radar. I wondered if that feature prompted him to go into the acoustics business.

"I'm pleased to hear it," I said, nodding. "I only want to use the best equipment."

"Too right! Sure, in the UK, I was just a little fish in a big pond, but out here, I'm a big fish in a little pond! Know what I mean?" At least his questions ended on a lower note.

"I think you mean that you can produce the right sound, no?"

"Too right, Mr. Santos. Or should I call you Carlos, eh?"

"Carlos is okay. As I told you on the telephone, I want a good sound system, the best I can afford."

"You've come to the right man and the right company!" He ran a big hand over his cranium's stubble. "As the name says, *Big Noise* is big."

I stroked my false moustache as if in thought. "That is what I want. But it must be within the right parameters, according to the safe recommendations, no?"

"Hey, you don't want to take any notice of all that so-called safety stuff. Statistics! In the history of the world, what did statisticians ever do, eh, I ask you?" He shook his head. "My equipment will knock your punters' socks off!"

I glanced at my feet. "Even if they only wear sandals?"

Atkins chuckled good-humouredly. "A sense of humor! I like that in a foreigner! The French, they're a bit too serious for my liking!"

"Thank you, I think."

"Right, then," he said, rubbing his big hands together, "let's talk specifications, shall we?" From his jeans' back pocket he pulled out a pen and a small spiral-bound writing pad. "Big question is, how much noise do you want to make?"

Many of my friends have grown up with noise. I was lucky, though I didn't see it that way at the time. My mother is English and, while on holiday on the Costa Blanca, she fell in love with a Spanish waiter, Paco. Apparently, it was a typical romantic fortnight that ended in tears, as she had to leave her lover to return to a boring job in Portsmouth. But the waiter followed her back to England. He hated the cold and what seemed like the perpetual rain but he persevered and courted her, even asking her father for her hand. He was accepted and actually got all of her, so they were married. In good time, they had a son, Juan, a daughter, Pilar, and then me, Leon.

I'm half-English, half-Spanish. The three of us spent some of our childhood here in Spain, but some in England, where it tends to be a bit quieter. As a youngster, I thought that wasn't so cool. I hankered after the loud and colourful fiestas, the big bangs of fireworks, the explosions and marvellous sights of Moorish and Christian pageants. It seemed to us then that everywhere in Spain was noisy and so much more vibrant and fun.

After over thirty years of democracy, there's little that has changed where noise is concerned. Neighbours, bars, discos, plazas, wherever people congregate or just live, they're loud.

Cars pass by with their stereos sending out an insistent deep bass beat, while bareheaded teenagers with helmets looped in the crook of their arms ride mopeds with high-pitched exhausts.

Angle-grinders and pneumatic drills seem ubiquitous in large tracts of my country, as if it was one huge building site.

Get two of my countrymen in a room and you'd swear they were having a serious life-threatening argument, yet all they're doing is passing the time of day, though speaking loudly. In fact, they don't talk, they shout.

It's the Mediterranean way, Pilar says. She should know, I suppose, since she married an Italian. Luigi makes good ice cream and he's a nice enough fellow—a good family man with two sons and a daughter—but he isn't in the Spanish league when it comes to talking in high decibels.

And yet, there are laws about noise levels, even in Spain. Of course, respect for authority is pretty far down the list for the majority of Spaniards. Many well remember those years under the dictator, when the walls had ears. Perhaps that was why people shouted—just to prove they weren't whispering and didn't have something to hide. Now, of course, I wonder if it's because they were deafened at a young age with all those marvellous fiestas.

A horn hooted outside. It was time for the delivery of freshly baked bread.

These days, I'm fortunate enough that I don't have to work for a living. A particular assignment enabled me to retire early with plenty of money, but that's another story. In the past, I've helped law enforcement organisations all over the world. Some of the work was clandestine, assisting the Intelligence Services. And I still have a few useful contacts, too.

As they say, travel broadens the mind. So, I can understand that Japan has the worst incidence of noise as they live cheek-by-jowl and are crazy about electronic gadgets. They are so inscrutable and serious about the concept of 'face'. And, of course, they gave the world karaoke.

Spain is the second noisiest country in the world and Madrid has been branded the most noise-polluted city in Europe. It's a pity, as our capital is an attractive thriving city, a place where I enjoy staying, even if it has to suffer all those politicians, many of whom haven't yet quite grasped the concept of democracy. Like all the great cities, Madrid has its parks, places to walk and take in the fresh air and get de-stressed. William Pitt the Elder said of London's parks that they were 'the lungs of London' and I believe that's true of all city parks, which enable us to breathe fresh air, isolating us from the stress and noise of the street and office.

Outside, the gas-cylinder delivery driver pulled up his truck and honked his horn loudly to advise customers he had arrived. Most homes still used *butano* to cook and heat water, though gradually mains gas pipes were being laid.

As the truck drove off, I said, "Just give me your top-of-the-range equipment, Mr. Atkins."

I could almost see him salivating.

Time to bring him down to earth. "It must be safe, though. I've heard that it takes the ear about thirty-six hours to recover after an evening of nightclub music."

Atkins shook his head. "There you go again, talking statistics! I've been in the business for years, Mr. Santos! I've helped set up so many gigs, sound systems and special effects and I haven't suffered! I'm not deaf!"

I felt like saying that I wasn't either, but the irony would be lost on him.

My friend, Felipe, ignored the rules while working on a building site and he needed a hearing aid and he was only forty-two. My neighbour Señora Aguilar suffered from irritability. Some say she got that from her interfering mother, high blood pressure and sleeplessness. She couldn't even hear the television turned up full. All because she worked in a nightclub for ten years.

The damage is self-perpetuating, as well. Televisions and music systems are turned up loud to compensate for impaired hearing. And, sadly, sufferers tend to become isolated and withdrawn.

"I'm new to this nightclub business," I told Atkins. "Have you any advice?"

"Charge high for the drinks, play loud music and set up some flashing lights! Oh, and have plenty of dark corners where no one can see what they're doing... Simple, really!"

"It doesn't sound very responsible, does it?"

"Hey, I'm not their parents! It's a hard life, you know?"

I nodded. "Still, a professor friend of mine in Barcelona told me that half of fourteen to twenty-seven-year-olds in his city are suffering from irreversible hearing damage. Doesn't that cause you some concern?" And of course that's not so unusual. The young of other modern cities will doubtless be the same the world over: deaf before their time.

He leaned forward, his bulk almost threatening. "Do you want to open a nightclub or a bleeding hearts' milk bar?"

"Oh, I'm in it for the money," I said, "just like you."

"That's more like it!" He rubbed his big hands together. "These teenagers need somewhere to rebel! Nightclubs and discos supply what they want!"

Of course, the young feel they're immortal, unbreakable. I did, too. I suppose it's the same with smoking. Because Tia Ana smoked all day every day yet lived to ninety-six, then you will, too. I remember suffering from an upper respiratory tract infection. That was abysmal, I felt like I was coughing up my lungs. Smokers can't seem to make that mental leap and see themselves in that terrible position, suffering, praying for the ache and pain to end.

Certainly, we all must die sometime. But it's the manner of our death that matters. Some ways are far worse than others.

In North America, men stressed with constant noise have been known to shoot their neighbours. From time to time I carry an automatic, but that, too, is a great responsibility. It shouldn't be used to settle an argument or to silence someone you find disagreeable. Tempting, though, I thought, sitting opposite Darren Atkins.

I can sympathise with anyone stressed by noise, whether it comes from a nearby airport, youths joyriding down the street in the early hours, or inconsiderate neighbours. When I lived in the Far East, the noise levels definitely got to me. Annoying noise all day and all night. That annoyance translated into anger, anxiety and even depression. Some nights I found it difficult to conduct surveillance operations and, as my work was affected, that just spiraled into dissatisfaction and utter helplessness.

I managed to get a transfer into the jungle for a couple of weeks. Isolation, with only the sounds of nature, worked wonders. Then I stayed with a group of monks and learned to meditate. After that, I adopted their meditation techniques at the first sign of stress.

"I must emphasise, Mr. Santos, that although we'll install sound-proof shields, which makes your place legal by the way, you don't want to be using them, not if you want to pull in the punters! You need to keep your shields up and doors open so they can hear the big noise blaring out! Only lower the shields at midnight!" He was beginning to sound as if he was on the bridge of the *USS Enterprise*. There was a warp factor involved in his attitude, anyway. He went on, "The neighbours can put up with it until then! You have a living to make, don't you?"

"Yes, of course." He seemed to have thought of everything. "That's sound advice."

"Hey, was that another joke you just made, Mr. Santos?"

"No, not really," I admitted.

According to the latest studies by people who Darren Atkins totally distrusts, noise levels above the sound of a vacuum cleaner will affect you, maybe gradually, but if it's persistent, then the damage can be irreversible. Tio Pepe suffered from heart problems and the doctor put it down to his working with heavy lorries.

I'd also be wasting my breath talking to Atkins about the clinical stress that persistent noise induces. Because he didn't want to hear all this. He sold and installed the equipment for the money. Atkins hadn't been affected by his diet of loud noise, had he? Too right...

***

Four weeks later and the *Big Noise* sound system was fully installed. Darren Atkins arrived outside just as darkness fell. "Hey, I thought you were having a grand opening tonight!" He gestured at the empty paved area.

There was a deafening throaty roar from a quad-bike as it passed, its sound bouncing off the buildings. Then, briefly, the sound of silence reigned, which was abruptly broken by an orchestra of crickets.

I glanced at my watch. "Later," I said, "after you've come inside for a surprise thank you gift."

He shrugged his shoulders. "Okay!" He chuckled. "A gift, eh? I don't usually get surprises from clients!"

"You'll appreciate this one, anyway," I said.

He followed me inside and we crossed the nightclub dance floor.

"Just stand there, Mr. Atkins, will you?" A red spotlight illuminated a circle in the centre of the floor.

"Okay! Do I need to close my eyes?"

"It might help," I said, and jumped up to the stage area. In a moment I slid behind the curtains and out through a door. I flicked a switch and all of the doors in the building were locked.

"What was that?" he shouted. "Hey, Mr. Santos! Can you hear me?"

I climbed the stairs to the control room and adjusted the equipment. Through the wide glass window, I watched Atkins standing under the red spot in the middle of the dance floor.

He'd opened his eyes and peered towards the stage area. "What kind of surprise have you got for me, eh? Dancing girls would be nice."

I picked up the microphone and announced, "I think the surprise will have a certain resonance for you."

"Was that another joke, Mr. Santos?"

"No, Mr. Atkins, not this time. Let me refresh your memory."

"There ain't nothing wrong with my memory! My patience is wearing down pretty damned fast, though, know what I mean? I've got places to go, people to see!"

"In that case, you probably remember the twenty young women who used to frequent *Agatha's Disco* in Southsea."

He whirled round and delivered a shifty look at the speaker on the left of the stage. "Eh, what're you on about?"

"That's the twenty girls that I know of, there are probably more. Only the parents of those twenty tried to sue you, and failed, just before you left the country. All those girls have seriously damaged hearing and now suffer from tinnitus. Half of them can't get a good night's sleep."

Arms akimbo, he sneered. "What's that got to do with me?"

My turn to shout: "And not one of them is over eighteen!"

He put his hands up to his ears. "Hey, turn the volume down, will you?"

I turned the volume *up*. "You built the equipment and installed it. Capable of churning out decibels as severe as a jet taking off."

Still with his hands to his ears, he shouted, "Those kids didn't have to go to the nightclub!"

"It was your nightclub," I reminded him.

"So? There are thousands of nightclubs and discos! Why pick on me?"

He had a point. There are plenty of similar establishments, and probably thousands of responsible sound technicians and nightclub owners. Voltaire came to mind. Mr. Atkins would serve as an example, to encourage others. "You didn't exert responsible use of your sound equipment, Mr. Atkins."

"Oh, come off it! They all want a good night out! Loud gets to them! I can't be held responsible for that!"

Louder on the dial: "Ah, *responsibility*. Nobody these days wants to know about that, do they? It's always someone else's fault."

He was whirling round in a circle, the sound of my voice bombarding him from all sides. He screwed-up his eyes whenever I spoke. "You're raving mad!"

"Yes, I am mad. Mad at you and people like you. I'm angry, in fact. If it isn't loud, it isn't good. What kind of measure is that?" If I entered a place where the music was so loud I couldn't hold a conversation without shouting, then I left. Their monetary loss, my hearing's gain.

I switched off the microphone and started the timer on the dials. It was set for twenty minutes. Enough, according to Jeremy, a friend who installs sound equipment.

Popular music blared, seeming to fill the building. I use the term 'music' advisedly. It was the neo-punk group *Vitriolic Paranoids*, and they sounded like pre-pubescent children who'd just discovered bass notes.

I thought I could see the glass partition vibrating with the sound waves. He'd be experiencing physiological effects from the noise now, the blood vessels in his fingers and temples throbbing, contracting, while the muscles in his arms would become tense. Temporary numbness would spread, too.

Atkins swore repeatedly as he walked unsteadily to the door and banged on it time and again. "I'll sue you for this!"

He would find that difficult to do, however. The premises in which he'd installed the sound equipment were vacant. 'Carlos Santos' had simply borrowed it with the owner's permission. And this morning a contact of mine hacked into Atkins's bank account and now there was no trace of any payment made by C. Santos. I had to protect my alias, as I would definitely be using it again.

Perhaps it wasn't politically correct to inflict on Atkins what he was happy to do to others, but somehow I couldn't see the parents of those girls caring about his discomfort. Besides, given time—according to Jeremy—Atkins's hearing would be no worse for the traumatic experience, unlike his 'punters'.

Leon Cazador, P.I.

In about thirty minutes, the law would clamp down on Darren Atkins as the soundproofing shields were automatically lowered and neighbours quite rightly denounced him and his offensive sound system. He would have a lot of explaining to do. Naturally, he'd mention me. Over the last few years, the police had heard of a Señor Santos, but he was a shadowy figure and had never been traced.

In the old days, I brought the ungodly to justice as often as I was able. Now, I still try to do the same, but on occasions, I simply give them a bit of rough justice instead.

Nik Morton

Leon Cazador, P.I.

PUEBLO PRIDE

"Esperanza!" I exclaimed. I picked up the packet of spaghetti she'd dropped as she bumped into me. "I haven't seen you in, my God, it must be ten years!"

It seemed to me that she hadn't aged. Such chance encounters can be wonderfully rewarding. It's pleasing to be recognised and remembered, after all. Shared reminiscences about the past. Discussing people, people who became lifelong friends or enemies.

"What a lovely surprise to see you, Leon," she said, smiling. All those years ago, I'd have given anything for her to smile that way at me.

"Did you become a doctor?" I asked. That had always been her dream. She was a single-minded individual.

"Yes, I qualified five years and two months ago."

"I'm really pleased for you." Esperanza was a dedicated soul and I felt sure that she would be popular with all her patients. "Is your surgery nearby? Perhaps we could meet occasionally for *tapas* or lunch?"

She shook her head and my heart sank just a little. "Although I would like to, that's not really possible. I'm only here to visit my aunt and normally I stay in the village. I have a practice there—in the country."

I hid my disappointment. What she said next brought back vivid memories of another old friend, who had helped me in several criminal cases. This is his story.

***

The entire population of Pueblo San Miguel de la Virgen—all two hundred and twenty of them—shunned their favourite son, Doctor Diego Santiago, for many years. It was not the first time in their checkered history that the occupants had all spoken with one voice, but their reasons for this had more to do with hurt pride than bravery.

San Miguel was more an *aldehuela* than a *pueblo*, though the population would argue the point. Founded by the Romans, it sat quite serenely in the mountains, some 2,000 feet above sea level, yet overshadowed by the Sierra de Maigmó's twisted peaks.

Thirty feet above the town was a twelfth century Moorish fort, its walls crumbling. From this vantage point, there was a splendid view of the valley where an ancient aqueduct traversed the fertile fields. White plastic bags scurried over the *alcachofas* like errant egrets. Household refuse and builders' garbage littered the slopes that fell away from the access road. To the right of the entrance arch was the electricity sub-station, its concrete and metal surfaces defaced with daubs of red, white and green graffiti.

In the grandly named *Plaza Mayor*—it was the town's only square—was an ornate small fountain and the bronze bust commemorating the town's benefactor, Cardinal Villena. It looked cool and welcoming in the shade of tall leafy date trees. Blue and white tiled benches were chipped and unsightly, and spray paint added to the general run-down appearance.

The Moors took the town in 720 and put their own stamp on the buildings and gardens. Many years later, in 1491, Villena and his Reconquest troops captured the town. But the townspeople pleaded with the cardinal to spare the lives of the Moors, as they had been fair and decent, permitting Christian worship in the church without hindrance. Impressed by the townspeople all speaking as one, Villena convinced the troops to let the Moors live and to preserve their architecture.

On the eastern corner of the square, the mosque was left as a monument to a great culture. Opposite, was the church of Santa Ana, whose clock tower was slightly crooked, its timepiece stuck at three o'clock, when the earthquake of March 1829 struck. The upheaval also destroyed the mosque, and all that is left now are two ruined walls and an ornate arch, on which from time to time perch a colony of jackdaws, their sooty black feathers evoking a sense of menace.

At the time, the population only amounted to ninety-four and the earthquake killed thirty-five and injured twelve. A mural of the event was painted on the wall of the church, above the altar, behind the statue of the patron saint, Iago.

Along with three other families in Pueblo San Miguel, the Santiagos could trace their lineage back to those Moorish times. When it was obvious that young Diego Santiago showed great promise in school, a collection was made to finance his education. He thrived on knowledge and studied medicine. Although he lived with relatives in the city, he visited his pueblo as often as funds and time allowed.

When he qualified as a doctor, the town held a special fiesta in his honour. Doctor Diego Santiago set up his surgery and home in a villa at the end of the town, just to the left of the public washing area. Within a few years, he had delivered twenty babies and gained the thanks and trust of all the townspeople. He had grown into a handsome, tall man with piercing hazel eyes and tawny hair tinged with premature gray.

But his inquiring mind could not settle for long in the strict confines of his little pueblo. He trained up a locum who enabled him to travel widely for months on end, studying all the time. He always came back to his practice, however, and was welcomed like a lost son each time he returned.

He also found time to use his expertise to help me unravel several murder cases, and I counted him among my friends. Unfortunately, my work regularly took me away from Spain and our contact towards the latter years became minimal. Sadly, that's the way of things in the modern world yet, whenever we met up again, the years rolled away and it was as if we'd never been absent in each other's life. He had that wonderful ability.

As Diego Santiago got older, he sometimes regretted that he had not married and had children. He had been betrothed to Luisa Torres, who belonged to one of the pueblo's old families, but it never worked out and she went abroad to follow a career in art. No, the line of Santiagos ended with him. He lived for his work and medical research. In these moments of introspection, he grew critical of Pueblo San Miguel and its people, but he kept his peace.

Then a few years ago, the catalyst occurred. Doctor Diego Santiago was the joint recipient of the Nobel Prize for Medicine for research into signal transduction in the nervous system. He had absented himself once a week for several months to help in that research in Alicante.

Pueblo San Miguel was overjoyed and the celebrations lasted for two days and nights.

On the third day, the townspeople congregated in the square to formally honour their very own doctor.

Diego Santiago stood up and spoke with a deep sigh of regret. "I have travelled the world and I still find peace and contentment here, in our humble pueblo."

The overweight mayor stood beside him and nodded sagely, jowls wobbling.

"But the more I travel, the more disillusioned I become."

More nodding in response. The modern world, it moved too fast, it wasn't surprising that the good doctor wanted to return to his home to relax.

"We are proud of our pueblo, are we not?"

"Yes, doctor," they shouted as one, "*claro!*"

"Then why am I so saddened by the way you treat it and the countryside around our pueblo?"

People exchanged looks of confusion and concern. What was the good doctor talking about?

Like many of his countrymen, for many years Diego Santiago saw beyond the dereliction and mess. *Madre de Dios*, they were interested in people, not buildings and roadsides. But it still irked.

Now, he said, "I have seen towns less pretty than ours, but they are well kept. They don't throw their trash, even their old kitchen sinks, down the hillside. They don't permit graffiti. Anyone causing damage of any kind to another building is dealt with most severely. They, too, have a pride in their town, and it shows. Why can't you do the same, I ask?"

There were whines of protest.

"This is our pueblo, we don't need telling what to do with it!" snapped old one-eyed Cesaro.

"Graffiti is thought to be artistic in some places," shouted young Paco, thrusting his hands deep into his pockets.

"They are not graffiti artists," said the doctor earnestly, "they're vandals!"

The mayor said, "We cannot afford to be always cleaning up the town."

"It is easier to go on as we have always done," said Emanuel, the town clerk.

"Then, you must go on as you have always done," said Doctor Santiago. "But without me." He looked around at the sea of faces. Many of these people owed their lives to him. The gamut of emotions written on their features ranged from confusion to anger. Some pointedly turned their backs on him and walked away. Within a few minutes, they had all drifted off, going to their homes until only the mayor was left.

"I am sorry, Doctor, but you have hurt their feelings." The mayor shrugged, close-set dark eyes looking down at his small feet. "We are a proud pueblo, you know full well."

The doctor closed his eyes, pinched the bridge of his nose and sighed. "It pains me to be critical of my own pueblo, old friend, but I felt it had to be said."

Looking askance at him, the mayor asked, "Did you really mean you are leaving us?"

"Perhaps." The doctor gazed around, sadness in his eyes. "I like it here so much..." Then he spotted a pile of builder's rubble on a corner. It had been there at least three months. Briefly, a raven landed on it and pecked at a rodent, the sun creating an iridescent sheen on its black feathers then the bird flew with its meal towards the mountains. "But my old eyes now want to look on beauty, not ugliness."

Studying him strangely, the mayor said, "The people, they will come round. I have tried to look after the town but, you know full well, funds are scarce."

The doctor laughed mirthlessly. "Yet you have enough to burn during the many fiestas, no?"

"Ah..." The mayor grinned. "Different funds."

Time didn't heal their wounded pride. After two days, Santiago realised that his patients were going to the neighbouring village or even the city for medical assistance. There was no doubt about it: they were blatantly shunning him. It was with a heavy heart that he packed his bags and put a *SE VENDE* sign in the window of his house.

His shoulders stooped under the weight of a lifetime of care as he walked to his old car. Doctor Diego Santiago didn't look back as he drove down the road and out of their lives.

***

Doctor Esperanza Perez drove up the Pueblo San Miguel road and was enchanted by the whitewashed walls and terracotta tiles mingling with the ancient ruins. Lilac-blue rosemary was in flower on the hillsides and also yellow broom.

An old concrete mixer revolved noisily and two workmen shovelled sand and cement into it. A pile of broken bricks and rubble cluttered the roadside. Another two men stood leaning on their spades, watching as she passed. They stared at her pale unblemished skin and the long black hair that billowed behind her in the breeze from the open window. She was used to turning a few heads, but it meant nothing.

Esperanza pulled in outside the surgery and villa, noticing a woman bent over the old stone trough, scrubbing at a sheet while a little girl played with a floppy doll beside her. As she got out of the car, she heard the *kek-kek-kek* sound of a peregrine falcon. Her mouth curved in pleasure as she spotted the gray and white streak in a high-dive behind the Moorish fort.

This was a far cry from her last practice in Cartagena, but she welcomed it. She was a young idealistic doctor and had bought the practice within a month of it going up for sale. She needed this retreat from a soured relationship.

An old man with a black patch over one eye sat on a white plastic chair in the shade under a tree, chewing pistachio nuts and discarding the shells over his shoulder, out of sight. A scraggly dog sniffed around the bole of the tree then defecated and scampered off.

Esperanza walked past a decrepit house and banks of soil covered with pink *hedionda*, which looked gorgeous but smelled terrible.

She had noticed the garbage on her way up, the unfinished appearance of the place, but shrugged it off, as it was no different than the outskirts of many towns and cities she knew.

The mayor personally welcomed her to the pueblo and, as time passed, Esperanza worked tirelessly and grew to know and like the people of Pueblo San Miguel.

Gradually, she began to realise that the townspeople were suffering from some strange affliction, an unusual ennui. During one of his visits to see her, the mayor told Esperanza about her predecessor, Diego Santiago, "the last of his line."

After he'd finished, Esperanza nodded in com-prehension. "I'm not a psychologist, but I think they are feeling guilt about their treatment of Doctor Santiago."

The mayor chuckled. "Guilt? No, I don't think so. Our town has been through invasions and a civil war and you think they feel guilty just about avoiding the good doctor?" He shook his head. "We've committed no crime. He meant well but his comments were ill-advised."

"We shall see," was all that she said.

Time went by but the strange malaise suffered by over half the pueblo would not go away. Subtly, Esperanza began planting ideas in their minds.

And those seeds bore fruit. For many years, the townspeople strove to clean the pueblo. They improved it until it became a model of its kind. Esperanza noticed that the mysterious affliction seemed to find less victims as more and more people helped in the good work.

"When he returns, he will be impressed," they said.

No garbage, no graffiti.

"He will come back soon, won't he?" they asked as the years went by.

Then one day Esperanza received some sad news and asked the mayor to gather the townspeople in the beautiful Plaza Mayor.

As if foreshadowing her announcement, the bells of Santa Ana church chimed.

A slate blue rock thrush abandoned the crags above and landed on the back of an immaculate tiled bench seat.

Then, after the people had greeted her, Esperanza explained, "I'm sorry to inform you that Doctor Diego Santiago died last week."

A woman cried. Another sobbed, "Poor man!"

"It has all been for nothing!" someone wailed.

"He never came back!" shouted one-eyed Cesaro, accusingly.

"He hasn't seen what we have done for him!" the mayor moaned.

Esperanza held up a hand for silence and, surprisingly, she got it. "What you've done to your pueblo you did not do for your good doctor but for yourselves. You can choose to live in a scruffy unattractive place or you can live in a beautiful pueblo that is the envy of many in these mountains. Now, because you cared, the countryside—your country, *our* country—is clear of unsightly garbage and even the derelict buildings are photogenic!"

The mayor beamed with pride and laughed.

"I have here," she went on, "a final bequest from Doctor Santiago. He left all his money to Pueblo San Miguel de la Virgen so that you can hold an annual feast day to Saint Iago and also improve the medical facilities here."

There was stunned silence. Then words of regret. Why couldn't he have seen their efforts? "Because we shunned him!" whispered an old lady guiltily. If only he could have spent his final days here, in his hometown. "But we as much as told him he was not wanted here!" bemoaned another.

Esperanza commanded silence yet again. "I can tell you that secretly he visited our pueblo about a year ago." She paused to let the gasps of surprise die down. "And he was pleased with what he saw. Doctor Santiago was very proud of his pueblo and you, its people."

She omitted to mention the final paragraph where Diego Santiago said that he was content in the knowledge that the people of his pueblo had taken Doctor Perez to their hearts.

Doctor Diego Santiago's Nobel Prize was put on display in a cabinet in the little *ayuntamiento*. The town remained spotless and the people of Pueblo San Miguel de la Virgen were justly proud of it and their favourite son.

Leon Cazador, P.I.

DUTY BOUND

A mountainous landscape populated by dragons strode out of the swathes of sauna steam and approached me. Hiroki Kuroda was tattooed over his entire torso and down to his wrists and calves. At a glance, he gave the impression that he was wearing long johns; instead, he was a walking exhibition of Yakuza body art. Ray Bradbury's *Illustrated Man* sprang to mind, but this was no fantasy. As a member of the Yakuza—a Japanese criminal organisation similar to the Mafia—Hiroki endured hundreds of hours of pain simply to show that he could. He waved with his left hand. The little finger was missing at the first knuckle.

"Thank you for coming, Santos-san," Hiroki whispered as he sat beside me on the wooden slats of the bench. He knew me by my alias, Carlos Santos, rather than my real name, Leon Cazador.

"It is good to see you after twenty years," I said.

"Eighteen, I think."

I bowed briefly, acknowledging his superior concept of time passed. "I didn't know that the Yakuza had an interest in the Costa Blanca."

Hiroki chuckled. "*Hai!* Still direct, I see. Even now, after all these years, I find your *gaijin* ways most difficult."

"There's a time and a place for courtesy and etiquette, Hiroki." My tone implied he should get to the point, but I was not so much the barbarian as to tell him so.

He bowed. "There are two families in this area."

"That's a lot," I observed. Each Yakuza crime family would comprise dozens of younger brothers and many junior leaders. "They must have kept quiet. The authorities know about the Chinese Tongs, but no Yakuza have shown up on Spain's National Police radar."

"Yes, they are being circumspect."

"Unusual behavior for Yakuza," I said. Unlike other criminal groups in Japan, the Yakuza have never concerned themselves with keeping a low profile. Their social clubs and gang headquarters were blatantly marked with Yakuza signs and logos. "Clearly, their tentacles are moving out," I added.

"*Hai*. To other Asian countries, the States and now even Europe."

The Yakuza must have noted the criminal gains being made by the Russkaya Mafiya and the Balkan syndicates, and decided to have a piece of that action.

Just what we need, I thought. "Why are you telling me this?"

"I carry the hardest burden, Santos-san."

I nodded, understanding. "*Giri*," I mused aloud.

Back in 1988, as a member of CESID, I'd been stationed at the Spanish Embassy in Tokyo. I was part of an international team working with the Japanese Criminal Investigation Bureau, and I'd been involved in several police raids on the *mizu shobai*, the so-called 'water businesses', the Yakuza's network of bars, restaurants and nightclubs. This particular place of ill repute had been just off the Ginza, and there was a lot of confusion as doors were battered down. Half-dressed people ran in every direction amidst screams and shouts.

And a few stood and fought with automatic weapons.

More by chance than design, I saved the life of Nyoko, who was in charge of the reception desk. I kept her safe under cover from her demented gun-toting colleagues, and afterwards she agreed to testify in court in return for immunity.

True to her word, Nyoko gave evidence then went into hiding. She was Hiroki's wife, and he suffered considerable shame at her betrayal of his crime family.

He offered his little finger to his boss as an act of appeasement.

My last night in Japan had been sombre. In my brief stay, I'd grown to like the country and many of the people with whom I'd come into contact, though I still found their culture and ways baffling. It was a year after that raid, and I was scheduled to fly to China and report on the growing unrest among the populace.

I'd sat on the balcony, watching the bright city lights while having a quiet drink. The lights were mesmerising, and I reflected on how many cities and countries I'd left for good. Regrets, a few. Memories, plenty. But new challenges always seemed to beckon. I was twenty-six and craved adventure.

My visitor entered my apartment, cracking the lock without a sound and moved like a shadow.

Even so, I'd sensed his presence, perhaps a change in the air as he moved; perhaps it was my training with the monks in the jungle. I picked up the remote on the balcony table and pressed the switch: the overhead lights illuminated the entire room.

He stood there, completely dressed in black, without a mask. His face showed no emotion, but it was not threatening. He wasn't alarmed at being identified.

"I am in your debt—a debt that can never be repaid," Hiroki said, and he bowed and left as suddenly as he had arrived. Even though his wife had shamed him, Hiroki knew that I had saved her life, and therefore he was in my debt. That debt is *giri*, the burden that is the hardest to bear.

"I cannot lift the burden, Santos-san," he whispered now, "but I can ease it." He wiped a flannel over his flushed face.

I let the sweat ooze out of my pores. One way to be rid of a debt was to eliminate the debtee. "How would you ease your burden, Hiroki?"

***

The Yakuza perfected the art of people smuggling a long time ago. They took girls from impoverished villages of the Philippines and bought unwanted girl-children from Chinese parents. But with the Westernisation of China, that source was not so plentiful. Besides, many of their clients desired young Europeans rather than Asians, and they found that these could be sourced from the mess that was the new expanded European Union, which was now awash with thousands of illegal immigrants who wouldn't be missed.

The Okudaira crime family had been quietly moving in on the Romanian and Bulgarian gangs in Spain and France, taking over their 'comfort workers'.

"Sex tours are getting more popular in East Asia, as you know," Hiroki explained, as he sweated next to me. "The Yakuza have their hands in that trade as well. Organising holiday tours to cities in Bangkok, Manila and Taipei, where special hotels offer every kind of fantasy."

The cost in human misery, disease and death did not bear thinking about. Once, bringing the ungodly to justice was my duty, now, it was a calling. This seemed too big for me, though. Out of my league. There was something else he hadn't told me.

I stood and wrapped a towel round my waist. "You have renounced your crime family, haven't you?"

"You are as perceptive as ever, Santos-san."

"An educated guess," I said. "So why are you really in Spain?"

He smiled, not a wholesome sight, and his dark eyes shifted from mine. "I have contacts everywhere. They tell me that Nyoko is being kept here against her will."

"When did you last see your wife?"

"Six years ago. Not long."

"She may have changed in that time."

"No. Her name means 'gem', and she is as un-changeable as a jewel. We are as one. I feel it."

Somebody entered the sauna. He unwound his towel and sat opposite. He noticed Hiroki's tattoos, and his eyebrows raised then he looked away. His body was flabby, he didn't appear to be a threat.

"I'm interested," I said and stood up. "Tell me more in the car."

Hiroki nodded and I left first.

**

On the outskirts of Alicante, near one of those immense *poligonos*, there's a warehouse, one of hundreds. Cars rather than lorries visited this particular warehouse on a regular basis.

Inside, it gave the appearance of a furniture outlet, with open-plan sections divided into several salons occupied by scantily clad masseurs and their clients. A staircase ran up to a landing and ten closed doors.

Two Japanese men in dark pinstripe suits occupied the salon opposite. Wearing short black cocktail dresses, a couple of Eurasian comfort women were fawning over the men in a studied, insincere fashion.

From the adjacent salon, I heard the whir and clang of pachinko slot machines. Two youths were waiting their turn with the hostesses. These people were exhibitionists. Those who required privacy went upstairs. Others lounged, smoking, drinking and popping pills. The place was pervaded with a sickly-sweet smell of cheap perfume, sweat, cannabis, and corruption.

Pretending to be a client, I sat with my back to the bar and sipped a very expensive, tasteless drink.

A few moments before, a number of prime suspects had entered the rooms upstairs.

I spoke into the small lapel microphone and, within minutes, all hell broke loose.

The raid was well coordinated between the *policia national, the policia local* and the *Guardia Civil*. They netted thirty-two illegal immigrant women, twelve very embarrassed clients, four Yakuza regional bosses and two Spanish strong-arm men. Also in the haul was ten kilos of methamphetamine, six pistols and a sub-machine-gun, a computer complete with an interesting database and two stolen BMWs. Before leaving the warehouse, I downloaded a couple of files to a memory-stick.

"The information was good," Guardia Diego Estrada said afterwards. "We owe you, Leon Cazador."

The world seems to run on favours and debts. Though not perhaps as formalised as the Japanese variety. "Glad to be of help, Diego," I said, shaking his hand.

As I drove away, Hiroki shifted in the well at the back and then moved to sit on the seat. "They should be able to close down the Okudaira Yakuza," he said, "now they have that database."

I tapped the memory stick in my left breast pocket. "Let's hope so, Hiroki."

In my Torrevieja apartment, Hiroki scanned the files I'd lifted on my laptop and a smile transformed his features. "I have the address."

"Good. We don't have long. Word will soon get to them."

"You do not need to come with me," Hiroki said. "My debt is large already."

I drew from my shoulder holster the Astra A-100 and checked the magazine had its full quota of 9mm cartridges. "I'll watch your back, Hiroki. Let's go."

He shrugged. "Stubborn arrogant Western barbarian!"

"That's me," I said, and we left.

It was only a short drive. I parked the car on a piece of waste ground—there's a lot of waste ground in Spain. We got out. Hiroki was ten years older than me yet moved like a panther, sleek and silent. I was behind him, but it was hard work to keep up.

Within secluded walled grounds, the two-storey six-bedroom villa was floodlit. They hadn't bothered with electronic surveillance because they employed cheap Bulgarian guards. I know they were cheap because none of them saw Hiroki until it was too late.

The door was unlocked and the lobby wasn't covered by any CCTV cameras that I could detect. Arrogance or carelessness? Nobody seemed to be living here, which was odd. The upstairs and downstairs rooms, appointed with modern expensive furniture, were empty.

I gestured at the door leading to the basement. Hiroki nodded and it offered little resistance to his lock-picks.

Stealthily, we descended the stairs and at the bottom walked along a short passage. I'd drawn my automatic, safety catch off.

Immediately in front of us was a door. It slid open and the strong scent of orange blossom floated to meet us.

Dressed in a gold-trimmed kimono, Nyoko was on her knees in the centre of the ornate room, sideways on to the door. Her hands were tethered behind her back with red silk. She turned her head as we entered and her gorgeous eyes lightened as she saw her husband.

A stout Japanese man dressed entirely in black stood behind her with a samurai sword raised. His features were flabby due to too much good food and alcohol. His black hair was tightly swept back from his forehead. He eyed Hiroki and let out a low guttural laugh.

Hiroki said, "Kaito Okudaira, you have brought your family low."

Okudaira cursed Hiroki's ancestors then said, "I have been waiting for you. So has your late wife."

The terrible meaning of his words registered as I watched the sword descend.

Before the blade could do its grisly work, however, two *shuriken*, or throwing stars, smashed into Okudaira's wrist and the sword clattered to the floor. In that same instant, Nyoko rolled out of the way and Hiroki pulled out a knife and dashed towards his wife's captor.

Bloody wrist by his side, Okudaira adopted a karate stance, ready.

Before their bodies met in combat, I fired my automatic once and Okudaira tumbled backwards, a hand grasping his wounded shoulder.

"Leave him for the law, Hiroki!" I urged. "His life is mine. Your debt is cleared, your duty done."

Hiroki stopped in his tracks and looked down upon the once fearful crime-lord. Okudaira's dark eyes glared defiance, and his lips curled in disdain. The knuckles on Hiroki's knife-hand whitened. Those few seconds seemed to stretch into a long time.

Finally, Hiroki turned to me and bowed. "Very well, Santos-san. I am duty-bound to accept."

Nik Morton

Leon Cazador, P.I.

TRAGIC ROUNDABOUT

"Uncle Leon, what is that lady doing sitting on the *glorieta*?" Jacinta, my eight-year-old niece, asked as she gripped the back of my driving seat.

Like most of the women who frequent our local roundabouts, she was attractive, highly tanned and toned, wearing a white tube to cover her prominent breasts and white boy's-style shorts. She had long black hair and read a magazine while sitting on the outside edge of the roundabout in a green plastic chair, long legs stretched out, the heels of her black boots resting on the metal crash barrier.

I glanced sideways at my sister, Pilar, and she shook her head, clearly not wanting me to tell Jacinta the bald truth. I could live with that. In the wash of life, truth often comes out gray.

"Oh, that's Florence," I explained. "She's waiting for her boyfriend."

"*Sí, claro*," Jacinta said, satisfied and I grinned, not reacting to the poke in my ribs from Pilar.

Recently a wag, who had signed himself as Dougal, christened this woman and those like her with the name Florence. There was no sign of Zebedee or the magic roundabout.

***

Zebedee was a fisherman, the father of James and John, who were recruited as disciples by Jesus. Historically, many children were baptised in Spain with religious names and Jesus Raimundo Jaen was no exception. Now Raimundo was eighteen, which is a troublesome age. He was trouble for his parents, and he was trouble for the girls. It was only a matter of time before he became trouble for the police, too. Raimundo was good looking and smart, not in an academic sense, but cunning and street-wise.

His parents were friends of my family and they had approached me about him. They wanted to know my fees and if I would take on the case. Politely and with regret, I turned them down, as I was busy on something else and, anyway, I tended to steer clear of criminal youths. Although I'm conversant in several languages, I couldn't keep up with their street lingo.

I referred them to Chico De la Fuente, who was one of several private investigators working out of Alicante.

Surprisingly, quite a few investigators were hired by Spanish families to keep an eye on their teenage sons and daughters. The rise in street crime and drug use was a real worry. If they were sucked into crime, the shame could be devastating to the family. At least, these families wanted to know what their children were up to, unlike many parents from my second home, broken Britain, who didn't seem to care.

So, I was a little surprised to see Raimundo driving a metallic topaz blue BMW 330Ci convertible. He appeared older than his years, with his long black curling hair down to his shoulders and glinting narrowed dark eyes. He sat in the gray leather seat, arms at full stretch, as the vehicle emerged from the imposing entrance of the villa that I was keeping under surveillance. Interesting, I thought. That car would cost well over €30,000.

It could be innocuous. Maybe Raimundo was simply a chauffeur or a valet for quality cars.

I was tempted to follow him but I couldn't. I was waiting for someone else to come out of the villa grounds.

Apparently, Arnaud Laurent owned this luxury villa and seemed to be rolling in money. I'd followed him here in his sleek gray Maybach 57S, a German car worth ten times the BMW. I was slightly surprised. Laurent was well known for his arrogant patriotism, except, it seemed, when it came to cars. I'd have thought he might have opted for the French-made Bugatti Veyron 16.4, which was at least a million euros. His gardener had told me Laurent had two other very expensive cars in his enormous garage, a Leblanc Mirabeau and a Mercedes-Benz SLR McLaren. By all accounts, he seemed to be a prime target for car thieves. Save that, he was one of them.

Laurent was handsome in a dark Gallic way. He was tall and tended to look down his aquiline nose at everybody. At last, he emerged, driving his Maybach again, his profile unmistakable.

I followed at a safe distance in my borrowed Lamborghini Gallardo 140E. It was unpretentious silver with black leather trim.

This kind of car got you noticed and that was the idea. After about five kilometres, he slowed down. He must have spotted me, or rather the car, in his rear-view mirror.

Then he hit the accelerator and vanished from sight round a bend.

My first instinct was to floor the pedal, too, but I decided against it. I knew what the awesome power under the hood could do and I didn't have to prove anything. Besides, I expected to see Laurent shortly.

I smoothly negotiated the bend.

As I expected, he had pulled into the roadside and was now gesturing for me to stop. I pulled in and switched off. Fleetingly checking my false moustache in the mirror, I got out. The heat outside was oppressive, and I felt my shirt suddenly become damp and cling to my shoulder blades and jacket, partly due to the heat, partly because my survival instinct was working overtime as I entered the final phase of this sting operation.

"*Ciao*," he said, grinning broadly. His dark brown eyes were alight. Covetous.

"Is there a problem?" I asked.

"*Non, non*," he said nasally, walking up to me. "I was simply admiring your car."

Hooked already. "Yes, she's a beauty, isn't she?"

He held out a hand. "My name is Laurent. Arnaud Laurent. I am a collector."

His hand was bony and the grip was quite strong.

"Santos. Carlos Santos. What do you collect?"

He put an arm round my shoulders and laughed. "Cars, Señor Santos. I collect cars like yours."

"I see." I eyed his car. "You're a wealthy man, Monsieur Laurent."

"*Oui*! I am lucky in business, that is all," he said, dropping his hold on my shoulders. I fleetingly wondered if he had attempted to check me for firearms, but I doubted it. He had no reason to be suspicious. Anyway, I wasn't carrying today. Usually, my automatic stayed locked up unless I knew I was going into some dangerous situation. International car thieves were dangerous people, but I'd been informed that Laurent didn't do his own dirty work. He could afford to buy muscle and hit men.

"Are you thinking of making me an offer for my car, Monsieur Laurent?"

"*Mais oui*," he said. "The thought had crossed my mind."

Buying instead of stealing? It was possible but doubtful. "Here's my card." The ink on the pasteboard was dry, freshly printed that morning, and the address was genuine enough.

"*Merci*," he said and turned back to his car. He flicked the card. "I will give you a call."

I waved. "Do that, *Monsieur* Laurent."

***

That night, they came for the Lamborghini. Two of them, slim-hipped, light on their feet, with a bagful of lock-picks. The *Guardia Civil* and I were waiting. They were caught red-handed and the *guardia* wrestled the pair of them to the ground.

Seconds later, I checked outside and was in time to see their getaway BMW driving off. A police car was in hot pursuit.

I shouted to the *guardia*, "I'll return it in the morning!" I jumped into the Lamborghini and revved out of there.

The road burned up under my wheels, and the night was clear so I could see that the getaway BMW was out-distancing the police car.

Within a few minutes, I overtook the police. They recognised me and waved encouragement. I left them in my wake.

The pursuit took us along the A7 then veered off before the lights and barriers of the tollbooths.

An articulated truck was negotiating the roundabout at the top of the slip road and the getaway BMW didn't stop in time.

It was a mess.

I pulled in to the side, next to a green plastic chair, and got out and ran across the skid-marks on the road to the middle of the roundabout where the BMW was upended, its wheels spinning. The driver had been flung clear and was lying on his back.

I recognised the attractive tanned woman from the roundabout. She was kneeling by Raimundo, giving him the kiss of life, her black hair draped over his face.

Within seconds, the police arrived and the ambulance was with us ten minutes after that.

***

Her name was Tasya and she'd been a nurse in Russia but she got mixed up with the Mafia. She'd escaped to Spain but had no decent paperwork so couldn't be legally employed. Now she worked on the roundabout.

By her prompt action, Tasya saved Raimundo's life. She visited him in the hospital and I suggested that she ask him to talk about his contacts. He was reluctant at first, but she convinced him. With his statement and those of the two car-thieves we'd caught, there was sufficient evidence to obtain a warrant for Arnaud Laurent.

Unfortunately, when the National Police arrived at the luxury villa to arrest him, Laurent wasn't there. And the garage was empty. He'd been tipped off. The surveillance cops were discovered bound and gagged in the nearby *barranco*.

Worse was to follow, though.

The next morning, Raimundo was found dead in his hospital bed. There was no doubt about it, his death was definitely under suspicious circumstances. When Tasya visited later that day, she was distraught, blaming herself. I assured her that if anyone was to blame, it was Laurent. Not her and not me.

Whispers confirmed my opinion. Word reached me down the grapevine a few days later that Laurent had been peeved over Raimundo wrecking the BMW and then talking to the police. I felt sure that it was Laurent's way of ensuring silence and loyalty.

One day, I knew, our paths would cross again. Next time, Arnaud Laurent wouldn't get away with murder.

***

The following week we negotiated a familiar roundabout again.

Jacinta exclaimed, "Uncle Leon, that lady's still waiting for her boyfriend! If I was her, I'd have dumped him by now!"

Only by superhuman effort did Pilar and I keep our faces straight. There was no answer to that.

As we passed Tasya, I gave her a wave. She smiled but there was sadness in her eyes. She didn't know, but I'd set in chain certain actions on her behalf and I hoped that soon Tasya would be able to get off her roundabout.

Nik Morton

Leon Cazador, P.I.

BURNING ISSUE

Landscape defines some towns and cities. And even the people and the small mountain town of Cocentaina were perhaps typical. So I thought, as I drove Jacinto Alvarez and his wife, Puri, along the A7 on our approach. The town had been under siege more than once in its history and I reflected that that was how the Alvarez couple felt right now.

In the passenger seat, Jacinto hugged the bulging dark leather briefcase to his pigeon chest and sweated despite the efficient air-conditioning. Puri was in the back, fingering her worry beads and praying.

The town sprawled outwards from the eastern slope of the Sierra de Mariola. Its historic heart still beat behind the modern facade of new apartment blocks and factory units that produced textiles and furniture.

The Alvarez textiles were almost exclusively purchased by the design shops of Amancio Ortega for transforming into the latest fashions in the Ortega Empire, for outlets such as Zara, Massimo Dutti and Bershka. Where Ortega was valued in billions, Jacinto Alvarez was close to making his first million. Which, sadly, made him and his family a target for the ungodly, and that's why he got in touch with me and told me what happened.

Now that ETA had gone relatively quiet, kidnapping was not so commonplace in Spain, unlike Sicily, any South American country or Mexico. Their sixteen-year-old son Adrián was supposed to be collected from school by the family chauffeur but the man had been delayed about ten minutes in a rare traffic jam. In that time, Adrián was snatched outside the school gates. The *policia local* officer on school duty had been distracted by a scuffle on the other side of the road so he noticed nothing unusual. The chauffeur finally arrived to find that all the children had gone.

In the two hours after Adrián's disappearance, Puri telephoned their son's school friends but none knew the whereabouts of the lad. She started to worry.

Then Jacinto received the anonymous phone call. "We have your son." The voice was gruff, its owner probably a heavy smoker. It was a commanding tone, and not for a moment did Jacinto doubt the veracity of those words.

Jacinto felt that he had been squeezed by a clothes press. All air was expunged from his slight chest, and he leaned against the wall, his legs weak. He was struck dumb.

"Do as we ask and he will be safe," the voice went on. "If you tell the police, you will never see your son again."

Realising that his hand was stiff because he was gripping the telephone too tightly, Jacinto tried to relax. But he couldn't. He attempted to speak, but his mouth was exceedingly dry.

"I will be in touch in two hours."

The line went dead.

A chill ran down Jacinto's spine. At last, he found his voice. "Puri! *Madre de Dios*! Puri!"

His wife hurried down the marble stairs, and he gave her the bad news. He had to support her as she almost fainted.

"We must call the police!" she mumbled. "They will know what to do."

He shook his head. "We can't!"

That's when he decided to call me.

He was lucky that I was in the office. I was between assignments, but even if I'd been working, I'd have agreed to help. We'd been friends for twenty years, and he vaguely knew that my work led me around the blurred edges of the criminal fraternity. He didn't say anything about the kidnapping on the phone but his halting invitation intrigued me.

In their spacious villa outside Cocentaina, Jacinto told me everything that had happened. He was adamant: "No police, Leon. I'm taking a risk talking to you, but I need help. I don't think Puri and I can get through this without help."

It seemed to me that this was a well thought-out kidnapping. The culprits had clearly studied the boy's daily schedule. They were bold and efficient, and during my discreet door-to-door canvas, it was obvious that there were no witnesses.

I was at their villa again when the phone rang with the kidnappers' demand. "Bring €50,000 in used notes to the Santa Barbara hermitage at five tomorrow night. Put the money beside the fountain. When we have the money, we will put your son in one of the cottages. It's up to you to find which one."

***

Now, we were returning to the town with the money. Jacinto was unaware that under my jacket was my Astra A-100. I hoped that I wouldn't have to use the pistol, but I like to be prepared for any eventuality where the violent ungodly are concerned.

There were two main sections of Cocentaina. The first was within the remnants of the mediaeval walls, La Villa, which is the historic Christian area, the site of the Duke's Palace and the convent of the Poor Clares, where you can look upon an image of the Virgin Mary that has been an object of devotion since 1520 when it was seen to weep twenty-seven tears. We were not interested in this part of town or its history. Adrián's mother had cried plenty of tears, anyway.

I parked in El Raval, on the slopes of the San Cristóbal Mountain, and left Puri with the car and her worry beads. This was the ancient Moslem section. We walked through the shaded maze of lanes and alleys that wound their way up the hill in terraces. Stored from the day's bright sunlight, heat radiated from the stone. The rank smell of clogged drains and rotten refuse wafted past us.

As we approached the narrow climbing path, we split up, as agreed. I kept to the concealment of pine trees and rocks and occasionally caught the most welcome aroma of rosemary blending with the pine. For one heart-stopping moment, I heard the soft rustle and sudden flight of a disturbed partridge, but it didn't give away my position.

Jacinto passed several fresh water springs that were surrounded by an apothecary's assortment of medicinal and aromatic herbs.

The thirteenth century Santa Barbara hermitage dominates the southern side of town. Jacinto walked into a cleared space with stone benches and tables for picnickers. In the centre stood a fountain and a *chimenea* for barbecues.

From the concealment of a cluster of holm oak trees, I watched Jacinto put the briefcase at the base of the fountain. He looked around warily then backed off slowly.

Nobody about, it seemed. It was the time of the *paseo*, and the town itself might be throbbing with strolling families, but there it was quiet save for the songbirds and the odd rustle of a hedgehog or a leaping hare.

Before Jacinto reached the edge of the clearing, a man emerged from the trees on the opposite side. He wore jeans, a black T-shirt and a beret. A blue neckerchief concealed the lower part of his face. He gestured at Jacinto with a snub-nosed revolver. It looked like a Llama Ruby Extra, which takes .32 Smith & Wesson cartridges. Not a particularly powerful gun. "Go back!" the man snapped. "I will call on your *móvil* when we have got away safely."

"My son... you said you would tell me where my son is!"

"Later, when we have the money safe! Now go, before I lose my temper!"

Jacinto nodded and took reluctant shuffling steps back down the hillside, once or twice glancing over his shoulder.

The masked man retrieved the briefcase, and I moved through the trees in parallel and followed him.

My main concern was for Adrián. It was not unknown for kidnapped victims to be returned unharmed, but my usually reliable gut instinct told me that these people might not be so scrupulous.

Beret, the man I followed, removed his face covering and stepped into another clearing. He waved the briefcase aloft, laughed and shouted, "It is done!"

Two other men carried guns in their belts. They sat outside a small hunter's cottage with its window shutters barred. A campfire sizzled with a roasting hare on a spit and sent up a thin trail of smoke. They ate from hunting knives.

I pulled out my pistol. About to break cover, I was stopped in my tracks. Beret, the man I'd followed, suddenly grabbed a blazing stick from the campfire and threw it onto the cottage roof. They all laughed and continued eating. My God, I thought, they're going to burn Adrián alive!

I didn't hesitate. Rushing out, I caught them by surprise. They stopped laughing. I shot Beret first, in the thigh muscle. He lurched forward and fell on his side on the ground. As the other two stood up and reached for their guns, I shot them both in the thigh. They were lucky, I guess, since I missed the femoral artery. As far as I was concerned, they forfeited their human rights when they callously put Adrián's life in jeopardy.

Ignoring their yells of pain, I rushed up to them and grabbed their weapons and flung them into the trees.

Then I turned and left them writhing in agony and rushed to the door of the burning cottage.

I heard shouts from inside.

I tried the door, but of course it was locked.

"Adrián!" I called. "It's Leon Cazador! Are you all right?"

"Yes, Leon, but for God's sake get me out!" He coughed. "I can hardly breathe!" He coughed again.

Fortunately, the cottage was isolated from the surrounding foliage or the whole area would go up.

"Keys!" I demanded of the wounded kidnappers.

Beret gestured at the trees. "Thrown away..." he managed between gritted teeth. "Not needed..."

I considered shooting him again.

Then I thought about blasting away the lock, but you need some kind of protection for that activity. Police use shields and a special shotgun to burst locks. A pistol's bullets could fly anywhere, even inside, and wound me or Adrián or worse.

I ran into the trees and found a hefty log.

Taking off my jacket, I wrapped it around the trunk to give me better purchase and started using it as a battering ram on the right-hand shuttered window. The windows would be weaker than the door.

It took about five minutes but it seemed longer.

Seconds after the window burst off its hinges, Adrián crawled out, coughing and gasping on the fresh air.

We both must have looked a sight, covered in smoke and sweat stains. The leaping flames had scorched my eyebrows and shirt.

A long time ago, the Moslems from Granada attacked and burned Cocentaina to the ground. Far from being discouraged, the surviving citizens rebuilt their town and earned the sobriquet *socarrats*, 'the scorched ones'.

Right then, I felt like one of those scorched ones as I phoned Jacinto and told him the good news. "You can call the *Guardia* now," I added. "And an ambulance for three kidnappers who got their fingers burnt."

Nik Morton

Leon Cazador, P.I.

LONLEY HEARTS

"I think I love him, Leon, but I don't trust him." Kate's hazel eyes glanced down at her *café con leche* as she fidgeted with the sugar sachet. The detritus of a good *menu del día* was spread before us, breadcrumbs scattered over the white tablecloth.

As I sipped my *cortado*, I guessed what was going on behind those evasive eyes. She felt she was betraying a confidence by talking to me. But something was niggling at the back of her mind and wouldn't go away. We've all experienced similar thoughts. Self-doubt. If it gets too bad, you end up being paranoid. Kate wasn't paranoid. She was just unsettled and unsure.

She was fifty-two and even though she had a good appetite, she'd taken care of her figure. Doubtless, she felt—quite rightly — that she shouldn't be on the shelf just yet. Divorce or the demise of a spouse can play havoc with your self-belief. In her case, it was the death of her dear husband, Luke. I'd liked him a lot, a wonderful caring man who'd met his Maker in his sixty-fourth year.

"Far too soon," he'd said towards the inevitable end a few months ago. "Been robbed of my pension before I could get it!"

Kate was lonely and craved companionship. She felt unloved and unneeded. We all have to feel needed in our lives if they're to have any worth.

So Kate needed me, in the guise of my alias, Carlos Ortiz Santos.

***

"Well, Mr. Santos, I'm sorry your marriage didn't *work* out," Sandra Lee said, smiling, which seemed an inappropriate facial expression to wed to her words. But she was selling a life transformation, after all. She had blue eyes, attractive freckles, red hair and the irritating knack of placing emphasis on odd words. We were the only customers in the bar and sat in a corner, next to the ice cream freezer.

"Since we moved out here six years ago, we'd been inseparable," I lied. Nervously, my forefinger combed my false moustache. "It takes a bit of getting used to. I get really lonely, you know?"

She leaned forward in her seat. "Yes, I do *sincerely*, Mr. Santos." She wore a khaki business suit, and under the wide lapelled jacket was a low-cut white vest that revealed enticing cleavage.

I forced a faint smile. "Call me Carlos. Less formal, isn't it?"

"Whatever, Carlos. But you don't have any difficulty *with* the language, do you?"

"No, I'm half-English, half-Spanish. But I'm not a great mixer, you know?"

"Quite. Well, many of our clients are not so gifted, Carlos. They *find* themselves suddenly alone out here and *unable* to speak the lingo. They *feel* isolated and incapable of coping *without* their loved one."

I nodded, understanding only too well. She was pushing all the right buttons for a bereaved or divorced client.

"That's where we, *CD,* come in." According to her brochure, CD stood for *Carpe Diem*, 'Seize the Day'. Kate told me she'd found out that they'd originally planned to use the initials STD but dropped that idea when her friend Lisa pointed out that it stood for Sexually Transmitted Diseases. The organisation's line was 'New Horizons, New Life, New You!' Promises, promises...

"I'm only after friendship and company," I explained.

"Of *course* you are, Carlos," Sandra said, patting my hand as if I was an infant who didn't know his own mind. Delving into her slim briefcase, she pulled out a sheaf of fliers and handed me one. "Our next meeting is at the Los Piñas Bar. Can you *get* to it?"

"Yes. I know it." I moved my hand away in case she felt like patting it while saying, "Well done, little Carlos."

Instead, she gave me a big smile, which suggested that I was about to win the lottery. "I think I may be able to arrange for a couple of ladies to *meet* you there."

Diffidently, I ventured, "Do you think I'll be ready to meet a complete stranger?"

Sandra chuckled and stood up, businesslike. "Marriage is like riding a *bike*," she said, straightening non-existent creases in her skirt. "When you fall *off*, you have to get back *on* again."

I got to my feet, slightly bemused by the analogy. "I'm not exactly looking for another marriage just yet, Sandra. I'm still hurting after I fell off the last one."

"Right, of *course* you are." She shoved her pile of fliers back into the briefcase then patted my arm. "But you can't shut yourself *up* and let it get you *down*. *In* my experience, meeting other people, our kind of people, is the best way to come *out* of yourself."

She hesitated and I felt grateful at the cessation of her homilies. "Oh, I almost forgot. I'll need the introduction *fee* in advance, of course."

She got the right emphasis there, I noticed.

"Of course," I echoed, and fished in my wallet and paid her rather exorbitant fee.

She produced a pre-printed receipt from her breast pocket. She was certainly sure of herself.

"See you Friday, then?" I said.

"Friday it *is*, Carlos!" Exuding charm and professionalism, she sashayed out of the bar, doubtless on another romantic errand of mercy.

***

The Costa Blanca was not alone in having the problem, but it did seem prevalent here. The problem affected expats more than nationals. They moved here as couples—married or not—and, because of unforeseen circumstances, the relationship didn't work out. It hit emotional meltdown due to a variety of reasons: savings started to haemorrhage thanks to the endless work needed on the villa or the deplorable exchange rate hitting pensions; the cheap and easily accessible booze altered personalities; the laid back lifestyle meant chores didn't get done; or simply the fact of the couple living together twenty-four hours a day became too irksome.

Hopes and dreams were tarnished or shattered, and the couples split up or divorced.

Then there were those poignant cases where a spouse died.

The end result was the same; each one had abruptly become emotionally unattached. They soon realised that picking up the pieces and finding friendship or companionship may be hard enough in the home country, but it was far more difficult in a foreign land.

Nobody in that situation should feel alone. Fortunately, a variety of groups existed who were able to help bring unattached people together.

Occasionally, though, there were a few unscrupulous individuals who took advantage of this kind of situation. Sandra Lee and her unprincipled CD associates definitely fell into that category.

On the allotted Friday, I found that the meeting was well attended and quite cheerful, and the ice was broken easily enough with wine. The bar was literally that, about twenty tables on one side of the room, and down the other was a long counter. In a half-hearted or even half-baked attempt at abiding by the new anti-smoking laws, the owners had decreed the tables were non-smoking but smoking was permitted at the bar. The entire ceiling was nicotine stained.

Sandra made gushing introductions. Seating arrangements at the restaurant ensured that everyone could chat to at least two new people, no mean feat. The charge for the evening was a bit on the steep side. Not all of us were rolling in money from insurance or alimony settlements, after all. At least, the restaurant owners provided plates for the bread, and separate knives and forks for each course.

Tania was blonde and sat on my left. She was a fifty-six-year-old widow and had made a great effort to look attractive, bristling with jewellery. Neither that nor her tan was fake. She began telling me her whole life story, from precocious infancy.

On my right was fair-haired Lucy, more reserved than Tania, in appearance and manner.

Tania was up to her thirtieth birthday party and showing no signs of flagging when I said, "Excuse me, dear, but I mustn't neglect Lucy." I turned and whispered to Lucy, "I don't think this is working, is it? Care to join me for a drink outside?"

She smiled and nodded.

Making our excuses, we grabbed our glasses and headed for the balcony. I felt a few eyes on my back, perhaps Tania's between my shoulder blades.

The balcony overlooked the urbanization that clustered on the hill. Streetlights and a few house windows glowed in the dark. Moths clustered round the balcony overhead lamps. We sat in wicker chairs at a small round table and sipped our wine.

Surprisingly, now that she was not with all the others, Lucy opened up and gave me a potted history of her life. She worked part-time at an estate agent's, though the customer base had dried up of late. Her husband, Tim, had left her to set up home with a swimming pool saleswoman. "She used to maintain our pool," Lucy said. "And I guess that's not all she maintained while I was out at work." She'd been separated from her husband for two months now and she was taking it hard. "It's the betrayal I have difficulty with," she said.

"I can sympathise," I said. I offered a clean handkerchief and felt a bit of a swine, pretending to be someone I wasn't. "Life isn't always fair, Lucy, no matter what politicians promise. It's never black and white, either."

"Don't I know it!" She went on to tell me about her experiences over the last two weeks. Although this period had been marred by the burglary of her villa, Lucy had been quite upbeat about attending other social evenings organised by CD where she met two pleasant middle-aged widowers, Chris and Alan.

"It didn't work out. Chris wanted someone to clean the house and cook his meals while Alan was only interested in sex!" She blanched. "My God, why am I telling you all this?"

"Maybe I make a good listener."

She eyed me with interest. "And, Carlos, what do you want from a woman?"

"Only the truth," I said. "Tell me about your burglary. By the way, my name is not really Carlos," I confessed.

***

Breaking into the CD offices proved easy enough. The filing cabinets were helpful, as were the contents of the wall safe. Using several names and addresses, I discreetly interviewed a number of CD clients, both male and female. A few were reticent, but others were more than happy to divulge everything, indeed more than I needed to know.

By the time I called in the *Guardia Civil*, I'd worked out that Sandra used a coterie of four men and two women, all pretending to be widowed or divorced. When they got to know their new companions, they were able to case the various homes and arrange for a burglary while they were together for a night out. That explained Lucy's break-in.

The coterie was not averse to blackmail, either. A few compromising photographs would not cast the grandparent in a good light, perhaps, so the grandparent paid up and kept quiet.

By far the most despicable individuals were the men who had been sweet-talking two elderly ladies to the altar. Needless to say, the prospective brides were not poor.

So, my involvement on Kate's behalf proved timely. A watch was put on Sandra Lee's six accomplices and within the week, the police nabbed a pair of them red-handed breaking into a villa belonging to one of the CD clients. That provided the excuse for the police raid, which was successful. The CD files, computers and contents of the wall safe were taken as evidence. Sandra Lee and her accomplices were arrested, among them Alan and Chris, failed suitors of Lucy.

Although we caught all of those implicated in CD, I had no doubt that somewhere else a similar group of the ungodly was toying with vulnerable people's emotions.

***

"I'm sorry I'm the bearer of bad news," I told Kate over our meal in the restaurant.

"Not to worry, Leon." She shrugged philosophically. "I thought Alan was too good to be true."

Remembering Lucy's comments about Alan, I decided not to enquire further. "I'm sure that his feelings for you were not entirely an act. Nobody could fail to be attracted to you."

"Thanks. I want to think so." Kate brushed moisture from an eye. "If only he'd been honest, he could have had it all."

I nodded. "Honesty comes with a price, Kate. Most of the ungodly are unwilling to pay it."

Leon Cazador, P.I.

PRICKLY PAIR

With great care, I held down the fruit with a fork, and using a sharp knife, I cut off both ends and made incisions lengthwise. Now I could peel the fruit with my fingers and not suffer the ignominy of being irritated by the sharp hairs impregnating my fingers. Prickly pears may be a delicacy, but you have to know how to treat them. Like people, really.

Milly, my eating companion, chuckled as she watched, her dark brown eyes glinting. Sensibly, she'd selected melon and Serrano. "Reminds me of our club's chairman and his wife, the treasurer," she said.

I swallowed and pricked up my ears. "How?"

"The Gambols—they're a prickly pair. Most members treat them with kid gloves."

"If they're not popular," I suggested, "vote them out."

She lowered her knife and fork and leaned back in her seat. "Ah, Leon, you know what clubs are like. Very few members want to volunteer for a committee post. Reluctance, lassitude or whatever." She smiled, thin red lips moist with melon juice. She dabbed with her napkin at her pointed chin. "Despite their attitude, the Gambols do get things done. Most of us don't want the hassle or the responsibility."

Milly was in her mid-fifties and quite an old friend. She used to work in the Ministry of the Interior as an interpreter but now designed house interiors—quite a leap. The career change obviously paid as she wore a designer label blouse, jacket and skirt, and her gold earrings didn't come from *Brigitte Bijou.*

Milly told me all about the Chairman of the Sundowners Club, Ben Gambol and his wife, Irene. They were in their late sixties. Both were quite wiry, with lived-in faces. They'd been in Spain for nine years and still refused to obtain their *residencias* or even register on the town *padron.* Far too many expats thought that announcing their presence on the town hall's list of residents, effectively the electoral roll, would leave them open to additional taxes and rates, but all it meant was that the area would benefit from extra facilities, including doctors, depending on the number registered. As far as the Gambols were concerned, they resided in Little England and the Spanish were just a nuisance factor they had to put up with while they enjoyed inexpensive booze, cheap fags and wall-to-wall sunshine.

Apparently, they'd been into one get-rich-quick scheme after another. Very early on, they planted several prickly pears in their garden, intending to refine the gel and bottle it to sell as skin lotion. But the idea never got off the ground, though the plants certainly did: their garden was overrun.

Their latest scam was to buy cigarettes in bulk and sell them at a tidy profit to UK visitors. Unfortunately, they tended to smoke their profits and constantly complained about their poor health.

They were well matched as a couple. Very little pleased them and their faces maintained a mournful expression throughout the day. Irene had some slight excuse as she had an unmentionable but oft-referred-to "medical condition" that necessitated her taking a daily dose of pills. Uncharitably, Milly suggested Irene might be better if she stopped taking the tablets.

As luck would have it, I had a chance to check out Milly's rather jaundiced view. Nobody, I thought, could be as bad as she implied.

***

The Gambols had reported a break-in at their two bedroom villa. I arranged to go along with the investigating officers, ostensibly to act as interpreter, and then I'd report back to Milly.

Accompanying Rico and Emilio, the two *Guardia Civil* officers, I noticed that the gatepost tiles announced 'Beware of the Dog' and depicted a Rottweiler. I rang the bell, which gave out a high-pitched bark. They'd opted for an ersatz dog rather than a real one. Not a deterrent to the ungodly, however.

There was a wooden shed on the right hand side of the villa.

Columbus had a lot to answer for. The balcony at the rear overlooked the forest of prickly pears.

"If you lot are anything like the Brit coppers, you're wasting our time," Ben Gambol said as he let us in the front doorway. "You might as well just give us the crime number now, and we'll get in touch with our insurers."

Entering the lounge, I translated for Rico and Emilio, making his greeting sound less antagonistic, though there was little I could do about the man's tone.

"Do you want a coffee or something?" Mrs. Gambol asked from the American kitchen. Old grease discoloured the wall tiles surrounding the hob. She looked really anxious, and I didn't think it had anything to do with the presence of armed *Civils* in their home.

"Thanks, black for me," I said, moving towards the counter that acted as a room divider. "And the *Civils* will have a glass of water each."

Rico and Emilio slipped on their latex gloves and checked out the patio door at the rear of the lounge. Shattered glass was strewn on the tiled floor. Fingerprint powder, digital photographs—the usual.

"Don't they have a civilian CSI department?" Ben Gambol asked me.

"Usually, but they stick to serious crime," I explained.

"This is serious to us," Gambol said.

"I'm sure it is," I conceded.

Rico withdrew his UV torch and stepped out through the patio door, breaking glass underfoot as he went.

While Ben Gambol hovered by the kitchen door, his wife nodded towards the two cops. "Why are there always two of them?"

I shrugged. "Two pairs of eyes work better than one. Actually, they're a good team. They usually get their man or woman."

"Oh, really?" Ben said. "That's encouraging."

"It looks like the thief entered your property from the front," I said, "and walked round to the balcony and broke in through the patio door."

She put my coffee down. "That doesn't take a genius. I only wish we'd put prickly pears at the front as well!"

The mug was hot so I left it. "They're certainly a deterrent. But you still have to get in and out, don't you?"

"Of course we do!" Ben snapped.

Irene added, "I was only saying, well, never mind. Aren't you supposed to have some forms for us to fill in?"

I shook my head. "The form filling has to be done down at the station."

"You mean we have to go down to the police station?"

"Yes." Sometimes, I wonder if my English is wanting. "We're simply conducting an investigation now."

"Well, those two are," she said. "You don't seem to be doing anything. You haven't even tried my coffee yet."

"I'm talking to you, Mrs. Gambol. That's part of the routine."

She flushed, the lines on her face more pronounced. She glanced at the oven. I could feel the heat. "I hope you won't be long," she said. "I'm making Ben's favourite."

"What is that, Mrs. Gambol?"

"Beef Wellington. Ben just loves it." Her husband nodded, eyes darting to the kitchen door. "Ben can't abide the foreign food out here, and it's really hard to get hold of proper vegetables."

"You have to know where to look, I suppose."

"You speak good English for a foreigner, a Spaniard," she remarked.

"I'm actually half-English, half-Spanish," I said.

"That must be a bit confusing," Ben added. "You don't really know what you are. You're not pure one or the other."

"Oh, I've learned to live with it. *Habla español?*"

"Pardon?" they both echoed.

"Do you speak Spanish?"

She laughed, a throaty sound, testament to a lifetime of smoking. "No, we've got our English shops and bars, and since they've opened the Chirpy Chippy Chappy, we don't have any real need to speak the local lingo."

You can't argue with that ghetto mentality, and I didn't try. "Can you show me the safe now?"

***

On the bedroom floor in the corner was an open safe, its door slightly askew.

"They used a sledge-hammer, I think," Ben said. "All Irene's jewelry...gone."

"Passports?"

"No," she said, "we carry them on us since we don't have *residencias* just yet."

"That's lucky. How much did they take?"

"Oh, I can give you the exact figure." Her voice held a hint of pride. "€12,600."

"That's a lot of money to hold in the safe."

"It belongs to the Sundowners Club. We have €27,000 in the bank account but we keep some in cash to pay for the specialty acts that we hire."

"And was an act due to appear at the club soon?"

"Yes. The True Tremeloes, I think."

"You're not sure?"

"Well, Ben organises that side of things."

"The entertainment," Ben explained.

"I'm the treasurer," his wife elucidated.

"Of course. Can I look at your account books, please?"

Flinty hardness entered her eyes. "I don't think so. You'd need authorisation from the committee, at the very least."

I pulled out of my inside pocket a folded sheet of paper. "Will this do?" Milly had arranged it as soon as she heard about the robbery.

Irene's fingers trembled as she read the authorisation. "The swine did this behind our backs!"

Her husband snatched the sheet from her, and his cheeks reddened and his eyes narrowed. He swore under his breath.

At that moment, Rico and Emilio came in to inspect the damaged safe.

Rico spoke and I translated, "Can you open your shed, sir."

"No can do. You haven't got a search warrant," Ben blurted out. "That's private, I'll have you know."

I glared at him. "That may have sounded like a question, Mr. Gambol, but it wasn't."

***

As the shed door swung open, Rico gestured with his UV torch, and I translated: "Mr. Gambol, Rico says you should have swept the fine dust from your patio and around your house."

"That's my job," exclaimed Mrs. Gambol. "And my house is always clean!"

Ignoring her, I went on, "The only footprints in the dust are yours, sir. You went out through the kitchen door, broke the patio door glass and entered your house through there."

"This is utter nonsense!" Ben snarled. "We were burgled!"

I pointed to a sledgehammer in a dark corner of the shed, lit by Rico's torch. "You used that on your own safe."

Ben laughed. "Utter nonsense!" His face was covered in sweat now.

Emilio's latex-gloved hand delved into a pail of damp sand and came up with a *Mercadona* bag. Inside were many used euro bank notes. Probably €12,600. He pulled out another bag, and this contained jewelry. His dark features scrutinised Ben.

"You also intended to make a false insurance claim," I explained. "Indeed, the *Guardia Civil* has recently made several arrests for this type of crime. One man has even gone to prison."

At that moment, Ben swore and darted for the shed door. My foot caught his, and he tripped. He stumbled forward, unable to arrest his headlong momentum and let out an almighty scream as he fell off the patio and among several prickly pears.

I winced in sympathy.

Every movement he made must have been agony.

I said to Emilio and Rico, "Point taken, I think."

Leon Cazador, P.I.

CRIMINAL DAMAGE

*G**uardia Civil* sirens wailed, coming closer.
Alfredo Benitez was slumped in the bulldozer's cab, leaning over the controls. His huge shoulders shook as he wept.

The machine's engine growled as I walked gingerly across the debris. "You'd better get down!" I called above the noise. "They'll be here in a minute!"

Raising his head, Alfredo nodded. Streaks of moisture had washed channels of anguish down his dust-covered cheeks. Switching off the engine, he surveyed the damage.

***

When the new urbanization was planned, it sent shock waves through the neighbouring town of Pozo de Abajo. Alfredo's home had been in the Benitez family for over a hundred years, but history meant nothing to the gray-suited men in the town hall.

Josip Paz was the mayor and just happened to be the cousin of the builder awarded the contract. It was quite plain to all that he didn't care what new laws were passed to appease the EU busybodies. By the time anyone did something about it, I suspected that Paz would be out of office and sunning himself on a Colombian beach.

Devious Pozo de Abajo town hall officials and their local builders had already carved up the land, disregarding the plight of the current inhabitants, who were Spanish, British and Norwegian.

Raquel Benitez was one of them. She was Alfredo's sister and, at eighty-four, she still ran the household like her mother before her, though these days she allowed the use of a washing machine and a television, neither of which ever seemed to get switched off. Global warming was a quite alien concept to Raquel. She was thin and short, about five feet nothing in her thin black canvas shoes, and her features were wizened.

Whenever I visited, Raquel would laugh at some joke or memory. Her laughter rose up from her stomach and gushed loudly past dentures she'd inherited from her father.

This time when I called by, she was not laughing. She sat in the lounge in an ancient mahogany chair, her back upright. Raquel's whole body suffered from a marked tremor, but this was her mind quaking, not the ground she had lived on all her years.

"Leon, old friend, it is good to see you again," she said, rough hands gripping my big shovels between hers. Her eyes were almost colourless, yet I felt I could still glimpse a slight sparkle of the young beauty I'd seen in her photos on the sideboard.

"You are well, I trust?" I said.

She shook her head and let go. "I cannot sleep, I worry." She waved a hand at a letter on the dark wood mantelpiece, resting against the heirloom clock.

"May I?" I asked, picking it up.

She nodded. "Read it."

The paragraphs were in Castilian and repeated in Valenciano. Not as flowery as many official letters.

"Then tell me what we must do," she said.

A tall order, I thought, as I waded through the jargon.

Thankfully, the Benitez home would not be requisitioned for the new urbanization, but the family would be required to contribute towards the infrastructure of the new dwellings. The figure stipulated was €200,000. The old English robber barons had nothing on these people. "What happens if you don't have the money to pay?"

Her lips trembled and her eyes glistened. "Then they will take our house as payment."

Valencia has a proud tradition, yet its politicians seem hell bent on pulling the autonomous region through the mire. They complained about the fall in tourism and the slump in off plan building, yet they were blinkered to the effects of the bad publicity caused by its diabolical land grab tactics.

It's times like this when I despair of my fellow Spaniards. We've always shied away from authority, whether that was under the Moors, the Hapsburg and Bourbon kings, or Napoleon.

After years of dictatorship, we have a healthy detestation of anything that smacks of restriction or prohibition, constraints that hark back to those immoral fascist times. In a lot of ways, we have much in common with the English, and I should know, being half-English, that we don't like being told what to do. I must admit, though, that my English friends seem more compliant of late, quite happy to divest themselves of many of their rights without protest or complaint.

"Raquel," I said, "you must take legal representation. Consult *Abusos Urbanisticos No!* They're taking the fight to these uncaring people. Laws are not meant to stamp on human rights. And you have *every* right to live in your family's property or be *fairly* compensated."

"Paz and his cronies are no better than those terrorists we hear about!" Alfredo said, stooping to enter the lounge.

We shook hands and hugged, and I eyed him grimly. "It will be a long, and perhaps expensive, process."

"I liked what you said about human rights, Leon. I think we should take our situation to the Court of Human Rights. I think that our homes are more important than some of the piffling cases they hear there!"

I nodded, tending to agree with him. Hurt pride in the office pales in comparison to loss of hearth and home.

"Our neighbours, the Fusteras, will lose their house if the builders go ahead," Alfredo added, pacing the floor. "Can you believe it? The road-widening plan will make their house illegal because it will then be within the five-metre limit between property and a road!"

"I'm no lawyer, but surely prior rights can't be trodden on?" It sickened my heart to see the stress in my friends.

Legal battles had begun, I knew, but the diggers had already started at the top of the valley. The marker posts and plastic orange net fences were in place, delineating the area of the new buildings and roads. The intended road would pass behind the Benitez home, taking away many square metres of their property, without compensation.

"I went to see the mayor in his nice new offices," Alfredo said. "After five minutes, I got words of regret and was dismissed. We stand in the way of progress, he says!"

Always, it seems, the main corrupting power in Spain is *el ladrillo*—the brick. Builders gain contracts and lucrative work thanks to the notorious machinery of *soborno*—bribery. Still rife is nepotism, cronyism and of course mutual favours. Nothing new there. While I'd been studying at Newcastle University, I heard about the T. Dan Smith and Poulson cases of the 1970s. But here in Valencia it seemed more blatant.

Not all building firms are culpable, by any means.

Alfredo was a builder, one of the many honest workers who had done wonders in our country. Ironically, one of his cousins was an architect, and he'd been awarded a prestigious prize for designing a marvellous, functional yet attractive sports complex. The relatively few corrupt builders brought disrespect to the many, and it irked Alfredo.

All I could do was sympathise.

We shared a drink, and then I left, knowing that the constant worry would gnaw at them, every hour of every day, every waking moment, and there would be plenty of those, for sleep would elude them until exhaustion took over.

How I hated petty dictators who, without any thought or feeling about the consequences, ruined people's lives with the stroke of a pen.

***

The damage Alfredo had caused now resembled a war zone. Rubble and stone blocks were stacked in jagged heaps, while electric cables snaked everywhere. A water main gushed, capturing rainbows in the spray. Dust was settling slowly.

Alfredo stepped down from the bulldozer cab. He gestured at his handiwork. "He deserves worse than this."

I nodded. Alfredo's bulldozer had sliced Mayor Josip Paz's large two-story villa precisely in half.

At that moment, the mayor drew up in his limousine with his wife. She appeared distressed, while he was red-faced, moustache bristling. He was about to storm over to Alfredo and me when two *Guardia Civil* cars and a van arrived. They pulled in and shut off their sirens.

As several *guardia* stepped out of their vehicles, I recognised Lazaro, who worked in the fraud section.

Staying by Alfredo's side, I hastily indicated the rubble on the left, where the study was laid bare.

Lazaro nodded, slipped on latex gloves and clambered over the debris.

On the edge of the severed concrete floor, Lazaro examined a large safe, its door hanging off one hinge.

"Señor Mayor," Lazaro called, "would you come over here, please." It was not a question.

Scowling, the mayor snapped at Alfredo, "I'll see you in court, damn you!" He walked unsteadily over the rubble. "You'll be done for criminal damage!"

Criminal damage, I thought. Quite like that advocated by bureaucrats similar to him under the guise of official documents.

Lazaro knelt by the folder of papers that had spewed out of the safe. He held them up and said, "Can you explain these, Señor Mayor?"

Mayor Paz stared, his eyes widening. "No, I've never seen them before."

"Your signature is all over these papers, sir. Incriminating papers," Lazaro said. "I'm arresting you for fraud, Señor Mayor."

"This is outrageous!" Mayor Paz exclaimed. "You've planted these here! I left them in—" He stopped, as he must have realised he'd already said too much.

When Alfredo had told me the night before what he planned to do, I tried to dissuade him. Short of tying him up, it was impossible. He was determined to make a strong statement and protest.

I reasoned that going to jail wouldn't help his cause, so I broke into Mayor Paz's council office. It wasn't particularly difficult. It didn't take me long to crack his safe, either.

It had only been a hunch, but it proved correct. The documents inside itemised all the shady deals Paz was involved in. He needed to keep track, after all. I hadn't been surprised, like many of his kind, he'd become greedy. Greed or hubris is their downfall.

Careful to leave no trace of my nocturnal visit, I took these documents, broke into the mayor's villa, and put them inside the safe in his study. Then I advised Alfredo which section of the villa to demolish.

Simple, really.

Nik Morton

Leon Cazador, P.I.

PIGEON-HEARTED

Fireworks in daytime are not particularly spectacular, but that doesn't deter my Spanish compatriots from setting them off. The clear blue sky was momentarily sprayed with silver and red stars as the single rocket exploded above the town square. Minutes afterwards, a profusion of colours darted above our heads, but this display wasn't the transient starburst of more pyrotechnics. The palette that soared in the sky came from garishly painted pigeons released from patios, balconies, rooftops, and gardens. In the next few minutes, the number of male birds increased to perhaps seventy.

"My prize bird has been stolen!" a man shouted from a balcony on the opposite side of the street. He gestured at us and added, "Pilar, tell your brother I need his help!"

Pilar leaned on her balcony's metal railing and waved acknowledgement. "That's Lorenzo Sousa, last year's champion," she said. "It seems a bit drastic, to steal his prize-winning pigeon, don't you think?"

Resting my forearms on the rail next to her, I smiled. "All part of the competitive spirit, I imagine."

This pigeon business, organised by the *Federacion Española de Columbicultura,* was highly popular. There were competitions at various levels: the *comarcal*, the *inter-comarcal*, the *regional* and *comunitat,* and eventually on to the Spanish championships, where the winner could come away with a prize of €30,000.

Pilar eyed me, her thin lips curving. "It might seem a bit tame compared to your usual cases, but are you going to investigate his missing bird?"

I shrugged. "Let's see what he has to say."

***

Lorenzo was stocky, with broad shoulders and chest. He wore a checked shirt, fawn trousers and espadrilles, and swaggered from side to side as he walked towards me.

We shook hands and I found that his were calloused, the grip firm.

"Thank you for agreeing to see me, Señor Cazador."

"I may not be able to help," I said, and offered him a seat next to mine at a table outside the café in the square. On the third floor apartment balcony, Pilar waved down at me. I smiled back then locked my gaze with Lorenzo Sousa. "Does this kind of thing happen often, I mean, birds being stolen?"

He sat and barked an order at the waiter. "No, it has never happened in our town before." He screwed up his face in thought. "I think quite a few birds were stolen from the Guardamar del Segura pigeon club a couple of years ago."

I nodded, recalling the case. The culprit had been a man from Cartagena. He'd also stolen racing pigeons from homes in Cartagena and Murcia. "Is your bird identifiable with a ring?"

"*Sí*, of course, Señor Cazador."

I shook my head. "You really should bring in the *Guardia Civil*'s nature protection group, *Seprona*."

Lorenzo sighed. "I thought about it, but that last time, they were investigating a large number of birds missing, about 120, I think. Perhaps just one would not be worthy of their concern."

"What's your missing bird worth?"

"Oh, about €500."

"That much?"

"*Sí*, Señor. They are valuable, especially if he's a winner." He hesitated, pursed his lips then added, "The thing is, I'm sure I know who has stolen my bird." He shrugged his shoulders and flung out his arms. "But I have no proof."

"Your rival in the competition, I suppose?"

He laughed. "In more ways than one, Señor!"

Intrigued, I said, "You'd better enlighten me."

"It is Felisa Cortez's fault. She won't make up her mind."

The waiter carried a silver tray cluttered with orders, lowered a *café cortado* and a large brandy to the table in front of Lorenzo, then moved away to another customer. Lorenzo pounced on the brandy like a bird of prey and drank the liquor in one gulp.

"Go on," I said.

"I wish to court her but so does Ramon Cepeda." He raised a finger to scratch his beaked nose and nodded, his shoulders hunched slightly. "She says she likes us both and cannot choose..."

"So you think Ramon Cepeda has stolen your prize pigeon?"

"Of course! It is obvious. He has scored second for the last two years. With my bird out of the running—or flying—he must have a good chance of winning."

"It's a bit too obvious, isn't it?"

"He won't be foolish enough to conceal the bird at his home, naturally. But he will keep him out of the way until the competition is over, I'm sure, then probably release the bird to—"

"Oh, Lorenzo, I've just heard!" An attractive young woman ran up to our table. Her face showed consternation, and a few lines briefly marred her forehead. "It is terrible!"

Lorenzo stood and kissed her on both cheeks. "Yes, dear Felisa, I am very worried, as you can guess."

She glanced sideways at me as I stood.

"My manners!" Lorenzo exclaimed. "Señor Cazador, this is Felisa Cortez."

"*Encantada*," she said, giving me her fine boned hand. Her eyes were dark and fiery, her long black hair fanned out and frizzy, as if she'd been caught in a storm and it had reacted to the static in the air. She wore a brightly coloured flower-patterned wide skirt, thick black belt and a white cotton top pulled down to reveal bare shoulders.

"Would you care to join us?" I asked, pulling over a chair from the adjoining table.

"Thank you, Señor Cazador." As she sat, her head slanted to one side. "Aren't you Pilar's brother? The detective?"

"Yes, but detectives work for the police. I'm merely a private investigator."

She smiled and clapped her hands together. "That sounds much more fun!"

"Sometimes," I said.

"Excuse me, Señor," said the waiter appearing at Lorenzo's side. "A lady asked me to deliver this to you." He handed Lorenzo a small sealed envelope, which was not addressed.

Lorenzo glanced in the general direction the waiter indicated.

"She didn't wait for an answer," the waiter said. He turned, tray held aloft, and glided towards another table.

"One moment, please," Lorenzo said to both Felisa and me. Frowning, he used a stubby finger to slit open the envelope. A single sheet was inside. He read it and his face blanched.

"What is it?" Felisa asked.

He handed me the sheet. It was typed:

I want €2,000 for the safe return of your pigeon. Meet me in the middle of the field behind the Benito Patatas factory. 8pm tonight. No police, no funny business or the bird goes in my pie.

"May I?" Felisa asked, arching an eyebrow at Lorenzo.

He nodded and I gave her the brief note. Then he glanced back at the waiter, clicked his fingers to beckon him.

"Oh, this is despicable!" Felisa whispered. Her eyes rimmed with tears.

The waiter stood at Lorenzo's shoulder. "*Sí*, Señor?"

"The woman who gave you the envelope, what did she look like?"

"Old, very old," said the waiter. "She had gray hair and wore a black shawl. She gave me the envelope and pointed you out to me, Señor. When I turned to speak to her, she'd slipped away."

"Old but sprightly," I offered.

The waiter grinned. "Exactly, Señor."

Once the waiter had departed, Felisa shook her head and used a lace handkerchief to wipe her eyes. "I don't know how you can joke at a time like this, Señor Cazador."

"I laugh at adversity, Señorita, that is all." I turned to Lorenzo. "You know the field?"

"Yes," Lorenzo nodded. "There's a single palm tree and a derelict house in the centre, and that is all. No place for anyone to lie in wait and observe."

"Your pigeon's abductor chose well, then. Will you pay?"

He glanced at Felisa, his face quite woebegone. "I have no choice."

She reached across the table and rested her hand on his. Their eyes met. He may have lost a bird, I thought, but he had won a heart.

***

Seated next to me, Ramon Cepeda pointed at the collection of gaudy pigeons occupying the tree in the centre of the town square. "See, Señor Cazador, my bird is doing so well!" He had every reason to be pleased. His purple, green and yellow pigeon perched on a branch next to the only female, and a lot of billing and cooing seemed to be going on.

A short while after the males were released, the single female—called a paloma—was sent out to flaunt and vex. The paloma was trained to avoid the males, at least at the outset, playing hard to get. On the other hand, the owners of the males trained their birds for quite some time, indeed since the male attained sexual maturity at three months. The referee would award points for the time each male spent in the air with the female and in the courtship routine.

Fights in mid-air were not unknown, and a few males had died in the fray. All's fair in love, it seemed. Which got me to wondering about Ramon.

He was a diffident sort of chap. Pigeon-hearted, even. Stammering slightly, he publicly announced that since his rival's bird was stolen, he would withdraw from the competition. But many vociferous townspeople overrode his timidity and convinced him to continue. He was easily swayed. I suspected that a great deal of money was wagered on the birds' performance.

"That was noble of you, Ramon, to offer to stand down," I said.

He shrugged, his eyes not moving from his pigeon. "I thought it the honourable thing to do."

"Just so."

"Can I... can I ask you something, Señor?"

"Of course."

"I would... Are you..?" He lowered his gaze to my face. His dark eyes danced, suggesting quick intelligence. "I would like to know, are you a friend of Lorenzo Sousa?" His black hair was naturally curly and unkempt. I wondered if his self-effacing nature had anything to do with his short flat nose, which had been broken some time ago. He tended to stoop, too, doubtless conscious of being taller than the average Spaniard, the impression not helped by the vertical stripes of his *piratas* and shirt.

"No, why do you ask?"

"It is only that I thought I saw you speaking with him in the square, at the beginning of the competition."

"I offered to help him find his bird. You might have seen Señorita Cortez with us. She was most concerned for the pigeon's safety."

Ramon flinched at hearing Felisa's name. Then he smiled and nodded. "I see, now I think I understand."

"I wish I did, Ramon. Enlighten me."

"You both suspect me. You think I stole his bird, no?"

I shook my head. "I'm not sure one way or the other." Then I caught movement out of the corner of my eye. "Look," I said, turning, "your bird has flown off, he's chasing the paloma!"

He groaned, eyes darting. "Yes and so are fifteen others!" He sighed and stood up. "When this happens, it becomes difficult to keep track of them. The paloma, she is cunning, drawing them away, intending to tire them out. Only the sturdy with stamina will win their chance at further courtship and points."

I noticed his gaze stray to the opposite side of the square, where Felisa sat chatting with a couple of female friends. She glanced his way a few times, but her face showed no emotion. His eyes glazed, and then he looked down at the tabletop.

Fanciful, perhaps, but I imagined I'd just witnessed the first cracks in a breaking heart.

***

From my vantage point on the main road's flyover, I could train my binoculars on the field. The occasional car or truck passed, buffeting me with its slipstream. Undeterred, I watched Lorenzo carry the small rucksack along the earth track towards the dilapidated building and its solitary palm tree in the middle of the tilled field.

A few minutes later, Lorenzo walked back the way he'd come, still carrying the rucksack. He was smiling.

As promised, I watched the place until it was dark, the sky filled with countless stars.

Nobody came to collect the money he'd left in the ruin.

I switched to night-sight glasses and spent four hours watching and was rewarded with a stiff neck, aching arms and a raging thirst.

Enough is enough, I thought. I lowered the glasses, clambered into my 4x4 and drove off the down-ramp. I parked at the edge of the field and locked the car.

It was easy enough to jump over the crash barrier and the narrow ditch that ran alongside the road. Then I walked along a raised portion of soil doubtless awaiting green shoots to be planted by the farmer.

By the time I reached the raised track and the ruined building, my shoes were considerably heavier, weighed down with clods of dark soil. I pulled out a small flashlight from my jacket pocket and searched inside the ruin. I was thorough, leaving no stone unturned—much to the annoyance of countless spiders, cockroaches, earwigs, and a couple of lizards. But I found no money.

***

Next morning, Lorenzo was allowed to enter his bird in the competition. "I know I now have little hope of him winning, but he so enjoys the tussle of courtship," he said, a twinkle in his eye. He was applauded for his gamesmanship and within a short time, his red, blue and white bird was edging away several suitors.

A handful of whisperers said it was unjust, since Lorenzo's bird had an unfair advantage. His wasn't tired out from flying and combating others for one day already.

"But," Lorenzo argued, "all your birds have had a whole day to amass many points, where mine has to begin from today!"

"So, the birdnapper got away?" said Felisa. She wore a bright yellow and green dress that displayed a modest hint of cleavage. She sat beside Lorenzo, her hand in his. Such public display of affection had an unsettling effect on Ramon, who sat next to me. She looked at Ramon and her lips curved slightly, almost taunting, as if signifying what might have been. Earlier, I'd arranged to meet Felisa and Lorenzo at the café in the square. I brought along Ramon without forewarning them. I felt a little like Poirot, assembling the suspects, though I doubt if my little gray cells would ever be a match for his.

"What's he doing here?" Lorenzo had snapped.

"Lorenzo, that's no way to speak to Señor Cazador."

"Sorry, my dear."

"As Ramon is the prime suspect," I said, "it seemed appropriate to ask him to join us."

"I—I wasn't keen on the idea, for obvious reasons," Ramon murmured. He glanced briefly at Lorenzo then away again. "I'm glad you got your bird back."

"Thank you, Ramon." Lorenzo turned to me. "It's a pity you missed the kidnapper," he said. He smiled at Felisa. "Not that I care too much for the money, you understand. I was happy to pay to rescue my bird."

Felisa's eyes lit up with adoration.

"As it happens," I said, "I did identify the kidnapper."

Felisa let go of Lorenzo's hand and leaned forward, her eyes wide. "You did? Tell us, please, who is it?"

"In a moment, Señorita," I said. I massaged my neck at the memory. "For many hours I watched that field. I saw Lorenzo take the payoff money to the ruin. Nobody else turned up, yet when I went down to investigate, there was no money."

"Just bad timing, I suppose. He must have taken the money while you were driving down from the flyover," Lorenzo suggested.

"That was a possibility I considered. Then I checked the footprints in the track."

"Footprints?" queried Felisa.

"The field had been recently tilled and the soil was moist, but the earth track leading to the ruin was dry as dust. I only noticed one recent set of footprints coming and going. Yours, Lorenzo."

Lorenzo let out a barking laugh. "Are you suggesting I took the payoff from myself?" He smirked.

"What?" Ramon said. "No, that...that doesn't make sense."

"It makes perfect sense," I said. "Lorenzo needed an impartial third party to witness the payoff. Unfortunately, he couldn't arrange a kidnapper for the pickup. I think he hoped that I wouldn't investigate too closely. After all, this case only concerns a pigeon."

"Is this possible?" Felisa asked Lorenzo.

He shrugged. "I don't think Señor Cazador knows what he's talking about. Footprints?" He laughed and leaned down, unfastened the Velcro of his left shoe. Slipping it off, he banged the shoe on the tabletop. "Here, check that out!"

"I have," I said, "and it doesn't match the print I photographed with my mobile phone."

"There you are then," Lorenzo said. He glared at me then turned to Felisa. "Ramon has put him up to this, I assure you, my dear."

"I—I would not do such a dishonourable thing," said Ramon.

Felisa's cheeks flushed, and she eyed Ramon then Lorenzo.

"However, Lorenzo," I said, "your gait betrays you."

"My *gait*?"

I nodded. "You swagger, and this is reflected in your footprints—the outside ridges of the impressions are deeper, more pronounced. The length of the stride is indicative, also. Ramon, for example, is taller and would place his feet some two inches further forward than yours."

"You still speak nonsense," Lorenzo said. "So you have proved it is someone short like me and could not be Ramon. It must have been someone else who has taken my money, eh?"

"I have a witness. Your Aunt Ines was happy to tell me that you asked her to deliver an envelope to you at the café. She was confused but thought it was merely some foolish love note."

"Love note?" Lorenzo laughed, pointing to his temple. "*Tía* Ines has senior moments, Señor. None of this will hold up in a court of law!"

"The only court of interest to Ramon, and I suspect, Felisa, is that of courting. And it is quite transparent to all of us here that you pretended your prize bird was stolen to incriminate Ramon and to turn Felisa against him."

"*Madre de Dios*, how could you?" Tears welled in Felisa's eyes. Abruptly, she scraped her chair away from Lorenzo.

Lorenzo's face darkened and he stood up abruptly, toppling his chair behind him. Glaring at me then Ramon, he spun round and stormed away across the square.

Tentatively, Ramon's hand reached out and closed over Felisa's on the tabletop.

She lowered her lids, eyelashes fluttering. She didn't pull her hand away.

I glanced at the gaudy pigeons hovering around the tree.

The purple, green and yellow male was cooing in mid-flight with the paloma. It looked as though there'd be no separating them now.

To all intents and purposes, the match was sealed and the competition was over.

Nik Morton

Leon Cazador, P.I.

INN TIME

Surveillance took longer than I'd hoped. By the time the criminals were arrested, I was two days late setting off for my cousin Ignacio's home in Zaragoza. As I loaded my suitcase in the Seat's boot, I rang him from my mobile phone to let him know I'd be there later. Just my luck, snow had started to fall in the north the day before I left and by the time I drove into the mountains it was lying quite thick, though at least the main road was clear, if treacherously wet and slippery. To make matters worse, fog descended, which further reduced my speed. Not the most auspicious start to the Christmas holidays, I thought, as the windscreen wipers beat a monotonous rhythm interspersed with squeaks of complaint at not being changed during the last service.

The road climbed and twisted and turned. Oncoming traffic headlights glared, shards of light reflecting from the wet windows, blinding. My heart lurched as I instinctively touched the brake, padded it gently, repeatedly slowing down. If I'd been driving a little faster or been inattentive, I'd have hit the rear end of the parked car, its blinking yellow hazard lights quite dim in the conditions.

I let the engine idle, the climate control wafting warm air over me. I was late and the weather was hell out there. Drive round and move on. Ignoring my better judgment, I fished in the glove compartment for a torch, turned off the engine, switched on the hazard lights, shoved the shift into gear and ratcheted the handbrake one notch more. As soon as I opened the door, I felt reluctant to brave the elements.

Still, I stepped out and, as if on cue, the snow stopped. Keen to take advantage of the respite, I hurried over to the car parked in front of my Seat. It was a Fiat Punto, and the interior light was on, the windows steamed up. I swore. Not the best place for courting couples, I thought, as I rapped my knuckles on the roof.

The driver's electric window lowered, and a young man peered out. "Thank God, you stopped," he said. "The car won't go and my wife, she's pregnant! I was taking her to the hospital!"

Leaning to my left, I shone the torch inside. Sure enough, she was half-lying, half-sitting on the rear seat. One hand rested on her bump, the other gripped the headrest post. She blinked and glanced away. "Sorry," I said and lowered the torch.

"We need to push your car off the road or it's going to cause an accident," I told him. "Then we'll see about getting your wife to the hospital."

"Yes, yes, of course," he said. "Thank you."

"When I tell you, take off the handbrake, and I'll push. Steer over to that piece of waste ground," I indicated to the right about ten feet away. "Should be safe enough there until you can get the garage to send someone out."

He nodded and I walked to the back of the car. I pocketed the torch and braced myself, ready to push. The road surface was firm enough, at least, to give me purchase. "Handbrake off!" I called.

Fortunately, this section of road was relatively level, not too steep. After a few seconds of intense effort and my shoulder muscles protesting, the car started to move forward, and gradually it turned off the road. The driver braked as the rear wheels ran onto the waste ground.

At that moment, a truck bore down on my Seat, its horn blaring, brakes squealing. It wasn't going to stop in time. My heart pounded as I backed against the Fiat.

The massive crunch was deafening, my car jammed under its front bumper. Sparks flew as the heavy vehicle dragged mine with it and slewed across the road. It demolished the crash barrier. My car and the truck tumbled over the edge, leaving only a flurry of snow in their wake.

My mouth was dry, even though damp white fronds of my breath filled the air. My flesh ran cold, and I shuddered. I'd been close to death many times, but the body never gets used to it.

I glanced at the expectant father. He stared in shock at the gap in the road barrier.

I took out my mobile phone, but there was no signal, weather or the position affecting it, without doubt. I enquired but the

Leon Cazador, P.I.

husband's phone was inoperative as well, so we couldn't alert the emergency services.

There was no more traffic, it seemed. I ran across the empty road and peered down, but there were no headlight beams, just blackness. I pulled out my torch and directed its shaft of light down the snow-laden mountainside, but there was no sign of the unfortunate truck driver.

Suddenly, there was an enormous explosion and flames briefly spouted up from where the vehicles had fallen off the mountain. I jerked back, turned my head away and in the fleeting flash of light, I thought I saw something that gave me hope.

Now, the snow started up again, but this time it came at us horizontally, driven by the *cierzo*, the cold dry wind from the northwest.

I moved to the other side of the Fiat and opened the door, slumped into the passenger seat. Grateful for the relative warmth, I slammed the door shut. I explained that we could sit in there and slowly freeze to death, or try to get to some shelter. "Not the greatest options, I know," I said, "especially in your condition, Señora."

"Maria Delacruz," she supplied. "My husband, he is Jacobo."

I hunched round and nodded. "Leon Cazador."

"But we don't know of any shelter," said Jacobo. "I don't recall passing a building for many kilometres."

"When the truck blew up, I think the flames highlighted a rooftop over there." I pointed down a rough track on our right. Maybe somebody lives there."

"They might have a phone!" Maria said.

"Very well, we'll risk it," Jacobo said. "But we must be careful, Maria."

"I'm not an invalid," she replied and opened the door.

***

The track sloped downwards. It led to a double gate with a chain and padlock, which opened to useful skills I'd learned some years ago.

Jacobo whispered, "How'd you—?"

"Don't ask," I said.

The slope continued for a further ten metres or so and curved towards a large two-storey building, its roof covered in snow. So, either they had good insulation or it was empty. The sign by the door read: *Posada del Belén*. Inviting enough, I reckoned and rang the doorbell.

While I waited for any response, I glanced around. The trees were already snow-laden, and the gardens were virgin white. I hoped there wasn't a frustrated writer acting as a caretaker with a penchant for axing doors. In a way, I was relieved there was no answer. I paced to the left. A bay window revealed a large lounge, an empty hearth and a wall mounted full bookcase. On the right, another window showed a bar area, a small dance floor and tables with chairs stacked on them. "Closed for the season," I said.

"What do we do now?" Jacobo wailed, one arm round Maria, shifting from foot to foot as if that would warm them.

In response, I picked the lock. Easy enough, in my business. "This way," I said. I shut the door behind us and was immediately grateful for the relative warmth of the place. The lobby echoed to our footsteps as we stamped to be rid of the clinging snow. Then I shepherded them into the lounge on the left. There were plenty of logs stacked to one side. "Let's get a fire going."

It didn't take long to warm the place. Maria removed her coat and lay on the leather sofa in front of the roaring log fire. Jacobo and I raided the kitchens and found in-date lamb in the fridge and made sandwiches. While Jacobo heated some vegetable soup, I checked out the rest of the building, in search of a couple of blankets for Maria.

The reception desk phone didn't work, which was frustrating. I pored over the guest book. The last visitors departed two months ago. I wondered how long the place had been left empty. It didn't have a musty or damp smell about it.

The inn seemed to serve as a hotel, too. It had eight double rooms, and the furniture in all of them was draped in dustsheets. In one wardrobe, I found a cache of weapons and explosives, but I decided to keep the discovery to myself for the time being.

"The baby, it's coming!" shouted Jacobo.

I raced downstairs and asked Maria about her contractions. She nodded and wheezed, taking great breaths, doubtless to fight the pain.

"There's still time to eat something," I told Jacobo. "But, sorry, Maria, you must abstain from any food." She didn't look particularly hungry, anyway. Her whole concentration seemed to be on the intermittent and quite crippling pain.

A couple of hours later, the signs were there. I told Jacobo, "Now it's time. Hot water, towels." He got up and obediently hurried towards the kitchens. I moved over to the drinks cabinet. Its lock was flimsy and I encouraged it to open. A small brandy seemed necessary. It was a few years since I'd delivered a baby, but I told myself it was like riding a bike. As long as no wheels came off, I thought.

***

In the event, some six hours later, Maria gave birth to a lovely boy, and the procedure was without any complications.

I left Jacobo with his wife and newborn while I cleaned up and took the washbasin, towels and cloths to the kitchen.

I was on my way back to the lounge when the front door was opened with a key. Most civilised, I thought. Two men and a woman stood in the doorway, all dressed in snow-covered leather jackets with fur collars and hoods, and jeans and boots with fur edges. I was surprised to see anybody. Their expressions reflected more shock than surprise. If they were the owners, I could understand that.

My sixth sense kicked in, though, and the hairs on the nape of my neck stood on end.

They exchanged glances with each other. The woman lowered her hood and demanded, "What the hell are you doing here?" Her voice echoed in the lobby. "Who are you?"

"*Hola*," I said, offering a smile. "We took shelter from the storm." I gestured at the half-open lounge door that emitted a warm glow. "It was an emergency. I hope you don't mind?" That last was probably from my English side, even if delivered in Spanish.

"Emergency?" she said.

"We've just delivered a baby. Come and see."

With some reluctance, the three of them followed me inside.

"Hey, Maria, Jacobo, we've got visitors," I said.

Jacobo stood up and Maria hugged her son to her.

I eyed the woman. "Are you the owners, then?"

"Yes," she said. "I'm Melita Reyes and this is my husband, Beltran, and my brother-in-law, Casimiro." She looked at the empty plates and glasses.

"We'll clear up and pay for what we've used, of course," said Jacobo.

Melita removed her gloves, pocketed them and moved over to the fire. "No need. It can be our gift." She warmed her hands with the flames.

"Thank you," whispered Maria.

Melita's husband strode over to her and tugged at her sleeve. He gruffly whispered something in her ear. She shook her head and shrugged her shoulders. "You go with Casi," she said, dismissing him.

He nodded, turned on his heel, and the two Reyes brothers turned and left the lounge.

"I'm just going to the kitchen," I told Melita. "Do you want a drink?"

She unzipped her jacket and sat on the edge of a seat by the hearth. She seemed intent on the mother and child. "No, thank you," she said, without looking up.

I eased the door back and was in time to observe the brothers climb the topmost stairs, two steps at a time. I sighed, because I knew where they were headed.

There was an alcove under the staircase. Here, I pulled out from my ankle holster the lightweight Colt Officer's ACP LW automatic. The Astra A-100 automatic was still in its shoulder holster, packed away in my suitcase, amidst the burnt-out wreckage of my Seat. I had an uninterrupted view of the door to the lounge and the foot of the staircase. I waited.

After about ten minutes, Casi and Beltran descended the stairs. Their hands were full with canvas bags and machine-guns. When their feet landed on the bottom tread, I stepped out, my gun leveled on their chests. "Is this the new version, eh? Instead of frankincense, myrrh and gold, you bring the babe explosives, detonators and bullets."

"What are you talking about?" Beltran snapped.

Melita emerged through the doorway. As she noticed my weapon, she reached inside her jacket.

"Don't," I warned. "I'm a good shot."

"You cannot shoot all three of us."

"I don't want to shoot any of you, but I can't let you leave here, either."

"This is our property, Señor. You have no right to—"

"You've no right to blow up people, either."

"It is what we believe in," said Beltran gruffly.

"Then it's about time you got a new belief system."

"We want self-determination and territoriality," said Casi, shaking the weapons he cradled. "This is how we will get it."

"No, it isn't," I said, anger rising. I had to control it, otherwise, I was liable to make a fatal error.

"We fight injustice and tyranny," said Beltran.

I swore. "Franco's been dead over thirty years, and our country's now a democracy. Open your eyes, and look around the world. If you and Melita ever decided to have children, no dictator is telling you to restrict yourselves to one child. You're free to follow any religion or none, without persecution. If you're law-abiding, you need not fear the knock on the door at three in the morning. You have drinking water on tap and shops filled with food. Cheap clothing is available for all. You can read any material you wish without censorship. Need I go on?"

"The government tramples on our aspirations!" snapped Casi.

"Your bombs kill innocent people," I said.

"They're not innocent," said Casi. "They work for the government. They're fair game!"

"Those murdered *Guardia Civil* men and women were fathers and mothers, sons and daughters. They were not government tyrants." I gestured at the lounge doorway. "Inside there, is a mother and baby. Innocents."

"What would you have us do?" Melita said, her tone quite sombre.

"Give yourselves up. Renounce violence. If your aims are just and legitimate, fight for them by peaceful means. Don't create orphans and widows."

Beltran laughed. "You'd have us surrender, for the sake of that one baby in there?"

"Yes," I said, "and why not?"

"It's absurd!" said Casi.

"Is it? Just over two thousand years ago, another baby boy came into the world to spread the word. Peace to mankind. His Word's been diluted over the centuries, maybe, but it still holds true tonight, today. This is Christmas Day, after all."

"It's just a baby," said Casi.

Beltran pursed his lips and looked at his wife. Her eyes were moist, and she nodded briefly. Then he lowered the weapons and bags to the floor.

"Your weapon, please." I held out my hand to Melita.

Carefully, she pulled the revolver free and I took it from her, shoved it in my pocket.

Casi swore. "This is stupid! We've sworn to fight together until—"

"Until one or more of you are dead?" I said and shook my head. "Your so-called cause has killed over eight hundred people, including women and children and maimed hundreds more, ruining so many lives. Lives that are for living." I could easily have been talking to godless killers, but I'd seen the look in Melita's eyes when she sat with the mother and child, and I believed her maternal instinct had been deeply stirred. And, strangely, these two men looked to her for leadership.

Melita glanced at the lounge doorway again then moved over to her brother-in-law. "Bury the hate and love life," she whispered. "It's a good belief system, I think." She laid a hand on his arm. "Please, Casi, let's try it."

Casi glared at me then flung his bundle to the floor. I flinched as the bag's contents made a noise but they didn't explode. Melita hugged him, her lips pecked his cheek, and then she went back to her husband's side.

"What will you do with us now?" she asked.

"Leave your munitions here. And when the snow stops, go and send an ambulance."

"Then we're free to go?" Casi asked.

"Go, yes," I said. "But on the way, bury the hate."

Melita nodded and held Beltran's hand. "Very well."

At that moment, Jacobo stepped out of the lounge. He trembled as he stared at the discarded weapons and explosives. "*Madre de Dios*!"

I nodded. It seemed an appropriate exclamation. "Maybe this time there won't be any death of the innocents. Let's go in and look at the Christmas child."

Leon Cazador, P.I.

GONE MISSING

Miguel García Hernandez had been missing a week by the time his wife, Beatriz, got in touch with me. He'd walked out of his apartment in Edificio Donna Ximena, saying that, on his way to work, he was going to drop into the *loteria* shop to claim his euro *reintegro* from *La Primitiva*.

José on the lotto desk knew Miguel as a regular and was adamant that he had not come in that day. Miguel was supposed to go to the La Mata villa of Señor Rafael Morales, to fit a wooden carport in his drive. A three-day job, he'd estimated, but he never arrived.

Beatriz feared something terrible had happened to her dear Miguel and it showed in her sleep-deprived, dark brown eyes and unkempt dyed-black hair. She was in her mid-forties, but seemed older since the clear complexion of her chubby cheeks was mottled after she had dried too many tears.

She'd been quite a catch. Her family had worked in the salt industry since the 1820s. Salt was another word for money in Torrevieja. Beatriz thought that Miguel was the salt of the earth, and she should know. In the middle of last century, Torrevieja was a small fishing village on the southeast coast of Spain that also thrived on "white gold", salt production. Today, Torrevieja exports a million tonnes annually. Twenty years ago, its population was about 20,000. Now it's a sizeable city with in excess of 100,000 residents, over half non-Spanish.

"Do you know who his previous customer was?" I asked.

Beatriz shuffled papers in the sideboard drawer, its shining top filled with framed photographs of their son and daughter and grandchildren and nephews.

Family is important to us Spanish. But there was only one picture of Miguel, taken at least ten years ago. Next to this was a carved bull and matador, well executed. I picked it up.

"Whittling is Miguel's hobby, besides gambling," Beatriz said, and continued to rifle the drawer. "Here we are!" She wafted a piece of paper. "Señora Astrid Hedstrom, a chalet," she said, giving me the address.

"Thanks." I pocketed it. "I'll try this later."

Beatriz leaned against the sideboard and looked up at me. "Leon, I informed the police, of course." She then shrugged.

That hunch of the shoulders expressed much. The police were stretched at this time of year and, besides, notices had been posted with the decade-old black-and-white photograph of Miguel. Some families never take photographs and this was the case here. Since their children left, their camera never came out, not even for anniversaries or birthdays.

There was little more the police could do. Naturally, the hospitals were contacted as a matter of course. No accidents or deaths had been reported, suspicious or otherwise.

In these types of cases, the trail soon goes cold, whether you're searching for a villain or a missing person. I should know, because in my time, I've worked for several law enforcement agencies around the world. Now, I'm sort of freelance. If I can bring justice to a few of the ungodly, then I'm happy.

Miguel had been an insurance salesman until he was thirty-five, when he'd decided he wanted to work with his hands, creating something. So he became a carpenter. He celebrated his fifty-second birthday a couple of weeks before he went missing.

I had to ask: "What mood was he in?" Sometimes bodies were washed up on the rocks further south—failed illegal immigrants, mostly, and, infrequently, the victims or even members of the Russian mafia.

Beatriz shook her head. "No," she said emphatically, "he would not contemplate suicide."

***

I tried the neighbours first. The police had already done door-to-door, so I didn't expect much.

No. 4, next door, was occupied by a German couple living together, which wasn't unusual in modern Spain—or anywhere else for that matter. Here, in this near-paradise called the Costa Blanca, you found couples starting out again. Everyone—with the exception of murderers, perhaps—should have a second chance.

With a ready smile and gray intelligent eyes, Emil Müller answered the door. He spoke only a little English and some

Spanish— "though I go to classes to learn" —so in German I explained why I was there.

I'm one of those fortunate individuals capable of learning a foreign language with ease: I grew up bilingual, speaking English and Spanish, and soon learned Portuguese, French, German, Arabic, Chinese, and basic Japanese.

Emil asked me in. His partner, Greta Kauffmann, stood up from the sofa and deftly muted the Eurosport television channel. On the coffee table was a chess game, halfway complete. White was being seriously threatened. "Who's white?" I asked.

"I am," Emil said ruefully. "Magnus, my old dentist, is my opponent here. Magnus Olsson. We visit each other's apartment alternate weeks."

"A long game, then."

"Sometimes, it is like extracting teeth, Magnus says. Sometimes, far too short! He may be twenty years older than me but his mind is sharp, quick."

I broached the subject of missing Miguel.

"Yes, I told the police," Greta said, "I saw him leave our block at 9:30 prompt Thursday morning. I was just going to the *Centro de cultura Virgen del Carmen* to give a music class." She gestured towards her violin on its stand behind the sofa. "He said *hola* as usual and moaned about his meagre lottery winnings. We laughed at that and parted at the street entrance."

Emil started speaking but suddenly it made no sense and his eyes rolled back. It looked as if he was having a seizure. He was a big man but, between us, Greta and I managed to manhandle him to the floor and placed him into the recovery position.

"Keep talking to him, check his airway," I urged, pulling out my mobile.

Within three minutes the ambulance arrived and two paramedics hurried in. They were calm and competent and gave Emil blood pressure and ECG tests. As far as Greta knew, Emil merely suffered from tinnitus. He smoked like a chimney, though.

While the paramedics were taking Emil away, with Greta set to follow in her car, the neighbours at No. 5 had come out, showing concern. They were English, so I was more comfortable speaking to them.

Eric Jordan was weather-beaten and in his mid-sixties, the cliché image of an ex-merchant seaman, with balding ginger hair and a salt and pepper bushy beard. Beside him stood his wife, Gladys, her tinted glasses covering cool blue-gray eyes.

"I thought I saw him outside the swimming pool on Saturday," Eric said, shaking his head. *El palacio de la Infanta Doña Cristina.* "I sometimes walk off the pain—if I keep moving, it isn't too bad." Like many, he'd come here to benefit from the climate and ozone, anything to ease the joint pain and stiffness of osteoarthritis. "Better here than old Blighty, any day!"

I agreed, adding, "You saw him almost three days after he went missing?"

"Well, I *thought* I saw him. I called out his name, *Señor Hernandez*, but he didn't answer." He shrugged. "Sorry, it must have been someone who looked like him."

As I was leaving the Jordans at their doorstep, I met Ludmilla Vasilev in the corridor; she lived alone at No. 6. She was a part-time waitress working in a pub-restaurant and had finished for the morning.

She was in a hurry, as she wanted to get changed and go to the swimming pool. A friend, Dolores García, was waiting below in her Seat *Ibiza*. Ludmilla hadn't seen Miguel, and suggested I try asking her boss, Patrick O'Keefe.

O'Doyle's Irish Pub was open and I grabbed a bite to eat. O'Keefe was sensible enough to provide Spanish *tapas* and food as well as fare for the British clientele. Halfway through my *albondigas con salsa*, I recognised a wiry little man sitting at the bar: Ciro Jara. If I remembered correctly, he was wanted by the police on suspicion of car theft. I made a quick call on my phone and then I eased up to the bar.

"Ciro, isn't it?" I asked.

"*Sí*, what of it?" His close-set dark eyes screwed up. "Do I know you?"

"You probably saw me in court. I got your brother, Diego, arrested a couple of years ago."

He made to move towards the door, but I restrained him, pressing my hand against his chest, pinning his back to the bar. I felt his heart pounding. "We're waiting for company, Ciro. Let's not disappoint them."

Leon Cazador, P.I.

He swore but didn't move.

A few seconds later, the two cops arrived. Chico Gomez and Isabel Soledad. Isabel was a stunner with a black ponytail. Ciro was about to make a fuss but I suggested he go quietly, adding that I'd go quietly with her too, especially as I'd fought her on the dojo and she's good. He went quietly, in handcuffs.

O'Keefe's live-in partner was a redhead, Bridget Brannigan, who'd taken over the shift from Ludmilla. Being an ex-teacher of French, she was proud of her French accent, which held no trace of Dublin in it, but I asked if we could speak in English. Adjusting her bifocals, she said that she knew Miguel. He came round Tuesday nights to play dominoes with two Spanish pals, Paco and Manuel, and a Dutchman, Johan Hoek. They had missed him this Tuesday, though.

Bridget was a survivor from breast cancer and knew Nurse Inma Escobar in Edificio Manumiso, where she lived with O'Keefe. "The police have tried the hospitals," I explained.

"Oh, of course," she said. O'Keefe was still at home in the apartment, catching up on sleep in readiness for tonight. "Call on him at 5:30," Bridget advised, "not before. As for his domino partner, Johan Hoek, at this time of day you'll probably find him on his boat, the *Full House*, moored at the *Real Club Náutico*."

***

It was a pleasant stroll along the Paseo Juan Aparicio with the rocks and stone benches on my left. A tourist couple were having their photograph taken with the sculpture of Bella Lola, who perpetually stared out to sea for her loved one. The *ayuntamiento* had worked hard to eliminate the mindless splurges of graffiti, but they seemed to be fighting a losing battle. Ethnic and handicraft stalls were doing brisk business. It was still too early for the evening *paseo* of the townspeople. Torrevieja is well endowed with squares and monuments but it is nothing without its people, and this city has managed better than many to integrate an amazing international mix, with restaurants to match.

As I passed the port entrance, I waved to Pedro on Customs duty.

Now, the Paseo Vistalegre is attractive and modern, but it wasn't too long ago that it looked as though it had recently suffered its own little earthquake. Then some vandal deprived the statue band of their trumpet; I know where I'd like to stick the instrument if I ever found the culprit. However, the band has now been re-sited and a new trumpet restored. Never let the mindless vandals win.

I turned left, and climbed the steps to the marina.

Halyards clanged against masts in the slight breeze. Johan Hoek was on his ketch, *Full House*, adjusting the after lower shroud. I mentioned Bridget and he welcomed me onboard. He was swarthy and overweight, with brown hair and a mousy moustache.

He motioned for me to take a seat in a folding chair in the well deck and sat opposite me.

While I explained the purpose of my visit, I glimpsed the moored decommissioned submarine, S61 *Delfin*, a tourist attraction. It reminded me of the time I was clandestinely landed a few years ago from a British conventional boat. But that was another story.

"Yes, Miguel is a gambler." Johan's teeth betrayed excessive smoking. "Just like me. Bet on anything."

"Does he have any money difficulties?"

"Don't think so. But we're all feeling the pinch of the crunch, eh?"

Just then I spotted a sailing boat entering the harbour, the steering position was behind the mizzen, so it was a yawl. The water was almost up to the gunwales. As I'd seen the same boat leave the harbour a few hours earlier during my mid-morning coffee and brandy, I wondered why it should be lying so low in the water now. Perhaps they'd landed a big shark.

"Excuse me, Johan, I must make a call." Walking to the stern, I phoned Pedro and he agreed to prepare a reception committee. It was not unknown for smugglers to leave their merchandise hidden on Tabarca for pick-up.

"Sorry about that. Is there anyone else I can talk to? Fellow gamblers?"

Johan nodded. "Yes, the *abogado*, Rafael Morales."

I knew Rafael. We trained together at the karate dojo. I'd have to cancel a session tonight, since I was working on this case, but I could take ten minutes out to talk to him there. Besides gambling, Rafael enjoyed playing billiards and watching bullfights. "Reminds me of the court-room," he said.

A bald man came up from below. He had leathery features and a Cadiz-style beard.

"This is Pavel Sokolov," Johan said. "He's staying on my boat while his house gets finished."

"If ever!" joked Pavel Sokolov.

I knew him. He was a rogue builder. Señora Mendez in Calle Ramon Gallud had issued a *denuncia* against him because she had paid for work he never even started. As he'd given a false contact address and phone number, the police hadn't been able to question him: he'd done a vanishing trick. The gall of the man, to live on the seafront here.

"Unfinished work—that's something you know about, isn't it, Pavel?"

"Eh?"

"I'm sorry, Johan," I said, "but I'm going to have to make a citizen's arrest."

Pavel's best defence was extreme halitosis but he succumbed to a little ju-jitsu manhandling. I persuaded him to accompany me to the police station, where he was charged with fraud and working without a licence.

So I had my martial arts workout, after all. I still went to the dojo.

Rafael had finished his session. He sat in the changing room, towelling down after a shower. He wasn't surprised when I mentioned Miguel's disappearance. "That would explain why he hasn't turned up." He brushed a hand through thick, tawny hair. "I telephoned, but his wife wasn't too helpful. In fact she seemed a little distressed..."

"Yes, she would be."

"Of course, I can see that now." He adjusted his glasses with mirrored lenses, remembering. "No, it wasn't a three-day job—more like a day. The wood was delivered and his tools are still there."

"What about the gambling in O'Doyle's pub?"

"Harmless fun. Miguel is good, he gives nothing away. Keeps things close to his chest."

That's the problem, I thought. Nobody seems to know what he was thinking or planning to do. It happens all over the world, though. For no reason whatsoever, men and women just up and leave their home and family. The majority are found within days. Perhaps the most famous instance is the missing crime writer, Agatha Christie. She was gone for about ten days in 1926. Her reason was stress, the death of her mother coinciding with her discovery of her husband's infidelity.

But by all accounts Miguel wasn't stressed. He worked most days, but chose the hours that suited him. Starting about ten in the morning, he stopped for a light lunch at two and started again at four, and went on for a couple of hours and then returned home to Beatriz. Exceptions were when he worked further afield on big contracts, usually extensive fincas in the countryside or mountains. Sometimes he stayed at a small hotel to avoid excessive travel, as his VW van was rather ancient.

The van was found while I'd been talking to Rafael. Beatriz phoned to tell me. She was very distressed. After I'd calmed her down, I got in touch with a contact in the police station. I learned that the van was discovered near Avenida Habaneras. Badly dented, bonnet crumpled, the offside headlight smashed, it was against a yellow kerb, but there are so many illegal parking transgressors that it could have been a month before it was towed away. The cop on the beat had put a sticker on the windscreen. My contact confirmed there was no blood and no sign of foul play.

Coincidentally, the van was found close to Edificio Encarnadino, where Roberto Ramos, the pathologist, lived. We were about the same age and, from time to time, he helped me unofficially with my investigations. I knew he was a keen chess player. He also whiled away the time knitting. It took his mind off the cadavers, apparently.

Like many streets in Torrevieja, there was a motley collection of apartment blocks, all of eye-catching design. It seemed as though no two were alike. The potential was there for it to appear an absolute mess, yet it didn't. Balcony rails were draped with washing, lines were strung between some blocks, other high terraces were filled with bicycles while some were festooned with plants. Clearly, many balconies offered a retreat from the wear and cares of the day.

Roberto answered the door with a Marlboro hanging from his lips. He had a dark complexion and was prematurely gray.

"A little tame for you, this one, isn't it?" he said, pouring a coffee for me in the kitchen.

"From time to time I help friends." I shrugged. "It's what I do."

"You're a saint, Leon."

"No, not really. I just like to get to the bottom of puzzles and problems."

"Well, I can't tell you too much about Miguel. Yes, I knew him and we met occasionally in the bar."

Roberto also enjoyed dancing and his current dance partner—'purely platonic', he hastened to add—was Astrid Hedstrom, Miguel's previous customer.

Small world, I thought.

I went round to Astrid's chalet and asked about Miguel's work, which he had completed the day before his disappearance.

Astrid was a very attractive silver-blonde in her mid-sixties, with hardly any facial lines and a creamy white skin. I soon learned that she was an ex-beauty salon owner. "No, you are mistaken, Señor Cazador. He only spent two days on the work. He was fast but competent. I have no complaints."

There was a pattern here, I could sense it.

I arrived at the Edificio Manumiso and rang the Olsson's bell.

Magnus was quiet-spoken and his wife, Hilde, was a perfect advertisement, with faultless sparkling teeth. "I'm semi-retired now," she said, "but I still run a few sessions per week."

"What do you do?"

"Sex therapy."

Sex—frustration, obsession or whatever—could be a cause for leaving home. Sex and money are two strong motivators.

"And before you ask, no, I can't divulge who my patients are."

That told me straight.

Magnus, the dentist and chess-player, smiled. "Thanks for helping Greta with Emil earlier."

"Have you heard from her?"

He nodded. "Yes, he had taken two contra-indicated medicines, which she didn't know about. He reacted badly, but he's going to be all right. They'll keep him in overnight for observation."

"Glad to hear it. Do you know anything about Miguel Hernandez, anything at all?"

Magnus shook his head. "I've seen him about, from time to time. Never noticed him much, though. Sorry."

"Well, thanks," I said and left. Outside their door, I checked my watch. Five pm. Half an hour, then I'd call on Patrick O'Keefe. But first I'd try next door. The nurse, Inma Escobar, lived here. The door opened to my knock. Fortunately, she was in off her shift.

I showed my ID. "I'm looking for a missing person, Señora Escobar. Can I come in?"

"Yes, Señor Cazador, of course, though I doubt if I can help you." She ushered me into a neat little lounge and shut the door. "Most missing person enquiries are directed at the hospital."

"That's been covered already." I did a double take as I noticed on her sideboard there was a familiar whittled bull and bullfighter. Plus some family photographs. I had to ask: "Who's the couple?"

"My cousin, Dolores, it is her wedding."

"They look happy. What's her husband's name?"

"Carlos García."

Miguel's double.

I smiled. "You've been most helpful already, Señora Escobar, but I wonder if you could give me a little more information..."

***

According to Inma Escobar, her cousin Dolores lived at the Edificio Encarnadino. I knocked on her door.

Miguel opened the door. He wore a faded green T-shirt, jeans and espadrilles. "Yes, can I help you?"

"*Hola*," I said, and introduced myself. "I'm working on behalf of Señora Beatriz Hernandez and I'm looking for her husband, Miguel."

His brow wrinkled. "Those names, they sound familiar, but no, I don't know any missing person."

"Who is it, Carlos?" called his wife, Dolores.

He turned his head to answer. "A private investigator, he's looking for a missing man." On the back of his neck was a distinctive birthmark.

"Why's he come here?" she said, moving into view.

"Can I come in for a moment?" I asked.

"Very well," he said, "but don't take too long. We're going out."

Leon Cazador, P.I.

Dolores walked up to him and held his arm. I introduced myself again.

"Why are you here?" she said, dark eyes wary.

"I'm looking for this man," I said, and showed them both the decade-old photograph.

The likeness was remarkable, even so. "But…" she stammered, "this could be you, Carlos…"

He wrinkled his brow again.

"I think we all need to sit down," I suggested, "and perhaps have a coffee."

***

It took a while and plenty of coffee to disinter buried memory and unravel the facts.

Miguel had met Dolores when he was an insurance salesman, and fell in love. Yet he still loved his wife, Beatriz. The relationship with Dolores became so intense that he changed career and married her. When with Dolores, he worked as a painter, often 'away on contracts'.

He always over-estimated the duration of his jobs so he could spend that spare time with one of his two wives.

That Thursday, his van had been involved in a minor collision. The other vehicle drove off, leaving Miguel disoriented. He'd knocked his head and all memory of Beatriz and his life with her was submerged. Guilt can do that. He'd obtained help from several passers-by to move his damaged van against the kerb, then he went home—to Dolores.

He was surprised to learn that he was a bigamist, while his two wives were shocked and considerably annoyed when they learned the truth.

It had been a long day. I'd been instrumental in getting a few ungodly to help the police with their enquires and I'd interviewed German, Spanish, English, Irish, Russian, Dutch and Scandinavian nationals, all of whom had tried to be helpful regarding Miguel's disappearance. It was interesting to see how they all seemed connected.

Elsewhere in the world there'd be ghettoes—Little Italy, and Chinatown, and countless other small 'nations', each maintaining their separateness within the greater city.

But here, in Torrevieja, whether by accident or by design, that hadn't happened. Here, I witnessed it daily, people from all nationalities rubbing along together and enjoying life under the Spanish sun.

Leon Cazador, P.I.

GLOSSARY

Unless otherwise stated, the words listed are Spanish with English translation.

Abogado – lawyer, solicitor
Agua sin gas – mineral water, non-fizzy
Alcachofa – artichoke
Aldehuela – small village
Amigo – friend
Ayuntamiento – town hall
Barranco – gorge, ravine
Butano – butane gas
Café con leche – coffee with milk
Cementerio – cemetery
Chimenea – chimney, kitchen range
Cierzo – cold dry wind from the NW
Claro – clear
Conejo a la cazadora – literally, rabbit of the huntress
Cortado – small coffee, with very little milk
Delfin – dolphin
Denuncia – report to the police
El Gordo – the big one, lottery
El ladrillo – 'the brick'
El otro – the other
Encantada – charmed
ETA – terrorist organisation (Euskadi Ta Askatasuna)
Extranjeros – foreigners
Feria – fair
Finca – countryside house
Giri – Japanese, debt, hardest to bear
Hectares – fields
Hola – hello
La Primitiva – one of several lotteries
Llobadío – wicked curse from a wolf
Lobadas – blood lust
Lobero – wolf hunter
Los rojos – the Reds (Communists)

Madre de Dios – Mother of God
Madrileños – inhabitants of Madrid
Menu del día – daily meal, designed for working man
Mercadona – Spanish supermarket chain
Mizu shobai – Japanese, "water business'
Móvil – Spanish for mobile phone
Nǐ hǎo – Chinese for hello
Oficina de Estadísticas – Office of Statistics
Padron – electoral roll
Paella – a Spanish dish that varies by region, such as paella valenciana comprising rice, chicken, prawns, peas, mussels, red peppers, tomatoes, onion, garlic, and saffron.
Paseo – walk, stroll
Patatas – potatoes
Persiana – external metal window blind
Piratas – three-quarter length pants
Poligono – industrial estate
Posada del Belén – Bethlehem Inn
Pueblo – town, village
Puta – whore
Reintegro – bonus win on lottery, usually 1 euro
Residencia – certificated proof of residence
Reyes – kings, wise men
Río – river
Se Alquila – to rent or hire
Se Vende – for sale
Seprona – Servicio de Protección de la Naturaleza (Guardia Civil)
Soborno – bribery
Tapas – assorted appetizers in restaurants and bars
Tia – aunty
Tio – uncle
Transición – transition from dictatorship to a democracy
Urbanización – estate built outside established town
Xiéxie – Chinese for thank you

Leon Cazador, P.I.

AFTERWORD

Despite the statement in the Introduction, these stories are fiction; though several are based on real events and real people.

My first story about Leon Cazador was as a result of a writing prompt in the local Writers' Circle in 2005. Many years ago, I'd been a fan of Leslie Charteris' *Saint* books and hankered after creating a modern-day version. The idea of outwitting the con-man, the crooked dealer and the deceivers in society has always appealed. 'Shattered Dream' was my first attempt.

At the time, I was supplying a monthly short story to a local English colour magazine, as well as articles and film reviews. The editor liked the Cazador tale so I decided to use him again – in 'Bitter Almonds', which was inspired by a true story of an uncontrolled fire that wiped out a farmer's entire almond crop. Sadly, the real-life story did not end as well as my tale; the farmer committed suicide.

By now, I appeared to be in the creative groove, producing a monthly Cazador story for the magazine. For consistency, I settled on using two-word titles for all the stories, often playing on words and meaning – for example 'Cry Wolf', 'Big Noise' and 'Grave Concerns'.

Estate agents – or as they're termed here in Spain, Real Estate Agencies – had their boom period a few years before the financial crash of 2008. At the time of writing 'Off Plan', they were still riding high, seemingly oblivious to the threatening clouds of disaster. It seemed almost normal for clients to hand over to builders thousands of pesetas (or later euros) in cash, silent money' that never appeared in the accounts or on tax returns. The term 'Off Plan' means that people buy a property sight unseen; it hasn't been built yet, but they have seen the plan and a show house, and commit financially. Our first purchase in Spain was done like this; the builder had to remove a fair portion of a cliff to make way for a row of apartments overlooking a golf course; it took a year longer than 'planned', too. As in all professions, there are bad apples who screw clients and get away with fraud. The subject seemed ripe for the Cazador treatment.

Long before the present humanitarian immigrant crisis hitting Europe, it was evident that hundreds of illegal immigrants were attempting to cross the Mediterranean to seek a better life; yet this was the time of al-Qaeda, too. It seemed probable that among those many immigrants were agents of terror. Now, of course, the potential threat is far worse. I wanted to balance the genuine immigrant against the individuals who hate the Western way of life, so I wrote 'Adopted Country'. After all, my wife and I were adopted by Spain as legal immigrants, obtaining residency, a Spanish driving licence and tax-residence too.

I'd read that a number of farmers were blaming the reintroduction of wolves for livestock fatalities; however, the true story was more complex. Hundreds if not thousands of dogs are abandoned in Spain – some of them let loose in the countryside to fend for themselves. A few of these form packs. In effect, wolves, like foxes, are their own worst enemy. 'Cry Wolf' was the result. On the plus side, there is a wide-ranging collection of animal charities, many run by expat Brits to re-home abandoned dogs and cats.

As the backstory for Cazador included work in several countries in his eventful career, I wanted to introduce characters from his past. Here in Spain, there are hundreds of Chinese shops selling hardware, clothing, and electronic goods, taking advantage of favourable trading attitudes that have nothing to do with the E.U.; there's also a proliferation of reasonably priced Chinese restaurants. Having been influenced by a handful of friends concerning China, and having trained in Chinese martial arts, I wanted to involve Cazador in a confrontation with the Chinese tongs, and 'Dragon Lady' was the intuitive leap to make.

'Pueblo Pride' evolved from observation; as one wag has stated, Spain will be lovely when it's finished. Unfortunately, although new house building virtually stopped post-2008, and it was rare to see any cranes on the skyline, now the building has resumed and continues apace. And with it comes builders' rubbish... This story

Leon Cazador, P.I.

was entered in the Torrevieja International Story Writing Competition in English and published in the subsequent anthology.

The plight of endangered species should concern all of us. If the extinction is due to natural forces, then that's the way of nature; if it is due to the encroachment or greed of humans, then that is another matter entirely. Spain's nature protection group *Seprona*, a branch of the Guardia Civil is continually apprehending traders of endangered species. I wanted to highlight their efforts, though using Cazador to do that in, appropriately, 'Endangered Species'. The protagonists in this tale will appear in a forthcoming Leon Cazador novel. My novel set in Tenerife *An Evil Trade* also deals with the products derived from endangered species, as well as people trafficking and modern-day slavery.

Contrary to popular belief, not all Spaniards have natural black hair, as 'Fair Cop' testifies; another play on words, with two meanings! This story was inspired by the age-old con; nobody beats the shell-man. Even now, they are still active with a hastily collapsible table and fast running shoes.

From time to time there are reports of drugs being washed ashore or confiscated at sea on small craft. Drug-trafficking is very prevalent throughout Europe, needless to say, and from a writer's point of view it has become a bit of a cliché. So if drugs are involved, the challenge is to deal with the human dimension rather than the drugs. Here, in 'Night Fishing' I attempt to show that nothing is black and white where Leon Cazador is concerned.

The expat population in Spain tends to be of a certain age; sadly, many a wife has become a widow, as actuarial figures tell us the female of the species lives longer than the male. Understandably, they require companionship and inevitably 'singles' clubs have sprung up to supply a means to that end. As we know from scandalous newspaper accounts, not all people professing to have a lonely heart have a heart at all. I wrote 'Lonely Hearts' with this in mind, with a twist.

Kidnapping in Spain is rare, but it does happen. I wanted to tackle the subject from a local aspect, as Cocentaina is not far from home. Also, Cazador needed to be in an action scene, so I wrote 'Burning Issue' – the issue being the abducted son, of course.

By now, I realised I had to explain how Cazador subsisted. Plenty of do-gooders managed on fees from clients – Travis

McGee or Simon Templar, for example – while others were independently rich. Having read that the Templar treasure was still unfound, and there was a strong possibility it could be here in Spain, I set to work on 'Relic Hunters' and everything fell into place.

Since the end of the Spanish Civil War, there had been an agreement, a conspiracy of silence concerning the atrocities and the many unmarked graves. In 'Grave Concerns' I attempted to cast an eye on this, as the veil was being lifted and mass graves were being unearthed and the dead re-buried. All war is terrible, but civil war is especially horrendous as it tears families apart. This story has been reprinted a few times; it seems to strike a chord: it still certainly affects me.

Since seeing Robert Mitchum in *The Yakuza* (1974), I had been interested in that Japanese crime-syndicate. And as Cazador had spent some time in Japan, it seemed I could bring them to Spain in 'Duty Bound', and enjoyed doing so.

Local and national papers in Spain highlight the corruption to be found in many town halls. Partly, this stems from the old regimes, where nepotism and kickbacks appeared to be the norm. Considering the transition from the dictator Franco (dying in 1975) to a monarchy, Spain has made enormous strides. Yet some old ways linger. And of course corruption has always been around, and doubtless will continue to plague public life. The land-grab issues in Spain have been vexing to many expats, so I combined the two issues in 'Criminal Damage'.

The title 'Tragic Roundabout' is obviously a play on words. The 'bookends' actually happened – names changed, of course! There's been a market for expensive cars for some years, stolen to order, and Spain has seen its fair share of arrests on this subject. As a roundabout was involved, it seemed natural to blend the two themes.

The prickly pear is supposedly an unwanted import brought by Columbus' crew from the New World. The plant liked the climate so much, it proliferated. Not surprisingly, though rarely, sometimes custodians of community funds go astray, and here I wrote about a particular pair, tongue in cheek in 'Prickly Pair'.

Noise is a serious issue. As attested by people living in flats or near pubs and discos. Not far from our home, a complex was built adjacent to a residential area, comprising shops and bars. It's doubtful if any plans were presented to the public to invite objection. While we are far enough away not to be bothered, certainly, the tempers of those neighbours frayed and the police were called in. All of the facts concerning noise pollution have been verified. Sadly, in 'Big Noise' the big noise responsible in the story ignored the facts – at his peril.

Over the years we'd seen multi-coloured pigeons flying about and often wondered about them. Eventually, we found out that the *Federacion Espanola de Columbicultura* is exceedingly popular and a lot of money rides on the outcome. I had to use this typically Spanish pastime in a story, so wrote 'Pigeon-Hearted'. You have to feel sorry for the female bird, however.

Having had a number of stories published in a local weekly TV magazine, I was asked to provide a double-page spread tale for the Christmas bumper issue. Naturally, it had to be about the festive season. A good number of Hollywood films have featured stranded travellers in a hotel in the snow; I opted to go that route with 'Inn Time', but with a hint of imminent violence and, naturally, a pregnancy and the Christmas spirit.

For quite a while I'd been mulling over 'a day in the life of Cazador' and this finally evolved into 'Gone Missing', where he snags a few villains and tracks down a missing husband with unforeseen consequences.

At the time that this collection was being published for a second outing, my publisher asked several of their writers to contribute a story for their anthology. I determined to blend Semana Santa, the invasion of nasty processionary caterpillars and the apprehension of one of UK's 'Most Wanted' men, the latter based on a real event, and settled on the title 'Processionary Penitents'.

Leon Cazador also appears in a minor capacity in the first two books of my 'Avenging Cat' series, *Catalyst* and *Catacomb*.

The Author

Nik Morton hails from Whitley Bay, Tyne and Wear, England. He joined the Royal Navy appropriately as a Writer and in 1986 gained an OU Degree. He has sold over 120 short stories and edited *Auguries* and five ships' magazines. He was the sub-editor of the monthly magazine *Portsmouth & District Post*, and also contributed book reviews, articles, artwork and 'The Adventures of Super Scoop the Penguin' comic strip. He was the Editor in Chief of a US publisher 2011-2013.

He is the author of 30 books. His latest comprise three psychic spy Cold War thrillers *Mission: Prague, Mission: Tehran* and *Mission: Khyber,* a modern vampire thriller, *Chill of the Shadow,* a crime thriller set in Tenerife, *An Evil Trade,* a cop-turned-nun crime thriller *The Bread of Tears,* a crime series about 'the Avenging Cat', *Catalyst, Catacomb* and *Cataclysm,* and a sci-fi double bill of novellas: *Continuity Girl* with *We Fell Below the Earth.* He is co-author with Gordon Faulkner (writing as Morton Faulkner) for a fantasy series: *Floreskand: Wings* and *Floreskand: King,* which will be followed by *Floreskand: Madurava.*

His non-fiction book *Write a Western in 30 Days* is a best-seller and is considered a useful guide for all genre fiction writing.

Nik is married to Jennifer; they have a daughter, Hannah and a son-in-law Farhad (Harry), grandson Darius and granddaughter Suri.

His blog is http://nik-writealot.blogspot.com and his author page is amazon.com/author/nikmorton

Leon Cazador, P.I.

Other Manatee books by Nik Morton

GIFTS FROM A DEAD RACE
... and other stories

Collected short stories – Volume 1
Science fiction, ghost, horror, and fantasy

Brave firemen still do their job though suffering radiation poisoning after a nuclear war; but to what purpose? Maybe a simple little thing can save the world from an alien plague. Then again, maybe it can't. The first murder in space – can it be justified? Are dogs and trees and children as innocuous as they seem? You decide. If you're going to burgle a house, make sure you know who lives there – or else. The credit crunch can only get worse – worth an arm and a leg, you say? Hijack that plane? Not a good idea... Stranded on an alien planet, you know there's something familiar about those natives... He found that out the hard way that drink and driving don't mix. Criminals should be nice to little old ladies, or else. A birth on the moon? Sounds marvellous, or then again, maybe not. He lost his memory – then found he was buried alive, reliving his life! What if you had to celebrate Christmas two days early? Would the children notice? He had the last laugh when the Doctor misused his incredible discovery. The plague waited thirty-six years to show itself, and then went global.

'Nik Morton's 'A Gigantic Leap' re-imagines a piece of Soviet history and wonders what might happen if the American paranoia about space-born germs had been justified. It's a gently told story, narrated by an old man who has seen too much in his hard life. Then in the last few paragraphs, the stress and alarm build up nicely. All of the international panic and national security issues occur in the background, though, so as not to spoil the calm flow of the story. It's nicely done.'

'Spend it Now, Pay Later' is an unsettling and timely story of a single mother caught in an economic depression who jumps at an opportunity to get herself out of debt and build a future for her daughter ... Morton has over thirty years' publishing experience behind him and this latest story - a taut, nightmarish allegory from first word to last - is proof of his highly honed craftsmanship.'

Nik Morton

NOURISH A BLIND LIFE
... and other stories

Collected short stories – Volume 2

21 stories - horror, ghost, science fiction, and fantasy

She was custodian of a dilapidated house – or was she its captive?

Maybe even unpleasant nasty little planets aren't Godforsaken. Sister Rose was a nun with a difference – she used to be a policewoman – but now she's encountering something strange, beyond her knowledge of crime and God.

What if you had the power to share thoughts with only one other person – and he died? You don't know what being alone is until this happens.

Stories about time, grief, hope, love, betrayal and courage. Asking 'what if?' questions and providing some answers. Ghosts, aliens, villains, time paradoxes, romance, and the end of the world. Some stories will move you, others will raise a smile or a laugh and several will probably make you think. Try them.

'I read a lot and like to think that I'm fairly hardened to the human experience. Your story *Nourish a blind life* however, moved me enormously. With a powerful understanding you avoided any mawkish melodrama. The ending, although sad, gave satisfaction knowing the narrator was soon to be free! Thank you.' – Eve Blizzard, judge.

Leon Cazador, P.I.

VISITORS
... and other tales of the Old West

Collected short stories – Volume 3

7 short stories from the Old West

Whether it's the Sierras of the 1790s or the Chicago boxing ring of the 1920s, or any time in between, the characters of the Old West can be found in these stories.

Gambling played a significant part, too, among the cowboys herding their steers, or on the paddle-wheelers of the Mississippi or in the proliferation of 'last chance' saloons throughout the west.

Conflict with the Indians was not always straight-forward, either. There were shades of grey – notably in the guise of the Apache called Gray Wolf.

Here, too, you'll find the harsh conditions of the slums in 1860s New York and the vicious gangs that roamed there.

Always, individuals attempt to rise above adversity and grasp the opportunities that the 'new land' offers.

Why not visit now and throw your hat into the ring, and take a chance and hazard all?

'One of the very best tales ... is 'Bubbles'. Within a handful of pages Morton presents three-dimensional characters that live and breathe and wander through the years like real people, and we're treated to a heartfelt overview of a friendship that spans the decades.
- From *Meridian Bridge*

Nik Morton

CODENAME GABY
... and other stories

Collected short stories – Volume 4

18 historical tales

We are all history. And these stories reflect that. The human condition is unchanging, no matter where you are or when.

In these tales we travel to wartime France in 1943 and 1944 to witness betrayal and heroism. The effects of this war can also be seen from the perspective of 1995, looking back to 1943 and a loving family. Another conflict was the English Civil War, and here we meet protagonists in 1645. Some conflict occurs behind the headlines, however, and can only come to light when secret documents are released. Here are two missions, in Turkey (1976) and China (1977). And in Tenerife in 1896 a deadly crime is thwarted by an unlikely duo.

History is not all about battles, fortunately. It also concerns people coping in a strange land, whether that's post-war Japan or the colonial days in 1830s Australia. Combatting the elements creates historical events, too, such as crossing the Atlantic before Christ or surviving a sinking troopship in that same ocean, or dealing with crime beneath the Indian Ocean in 1965.

Political upheaval has its part in history, naturally, and the building of the Berlin Wall is hugely significant – as was its fall in 1989. The politics of mystic John Dee meant his imprisonment in the Tower of London in 1555, yet he survived by wit and guile. The London of 1857 signified the honouring of heroes by Queen Victoria.

In these pages you'll meet more heroes – and heroines – than villains. Travel far and wide, in the past and across oceans, in eighteen varied stories.

'('Codename Gaby') captures suspense, drama and wonderful character depiction. In less than 2,500 words, we know and relate to our heroine, the period and her situation. The story is complete and compelling. It is a remarkable achievement and demonstrates this author's outstanding writing skills.' – *Book Awards* reviewer

Leon Cazador, P.I.

I CELEBRATE MYSELF
... and other stories

Collected short stories – Volume 5

24 tales of crime and adventure!

Many kinds of crime are committed in these pages.

Hijacking a plane – or even a hovercraft – creates problems not only for those hijacked!

Crooks come in all shapes and sizes – from the petty to the bold. Occasionally, however, the individuals doing the stealing have good motives...

Borough council chicanery rubs shoulders with business betrayal.

Spies face incapacitating poisons and death.

Private eyes tread the mean streets, righting wrongs and investigating dodgy birth rights.

Here you'll find Mafia hoods, murderous hoodlums, and disgruntled book critics.

Besides death and destruction, you'll encounter humorous and uplifting stories.

Beware, though, some of these stories are not for the faint-hearted!

'*I Celebrate Myself*: ... story shares a keen awareness of social and economic plights that are empathetic rather than didactic, as well as a brooding anxiety over the fate of the next generation. In Morton's latest story, a police officer is called to dig through a trash compactor in the projects after someone claims to have heard a baby crying inside. Vividly caressed details make the characters and situation all the more real and relatable.'

Nik Morton

MISSION: PRAGUE

Tana Standish, Psychic Spy
in Czechoslovakia, 1975

It's 1975 and Czechoslovakia's people are still kicking against the Soviet invasion.

Tana Standish, a British psychic spy, is called in to repair the underground network.

But there's a traitor at work.

And there's an establishment in Kazakhstan, where Yakunin, one of their gifted psychics, has detected her presence in Czechoslovakia. As he gets to know her, his loyalties become strained: does he hunt her or save her?

When Tana's captured in a secret Soviet complex, London sends in Keith Tyson in a desperate attempt to get her out - or to silence her - before she breaks under interrogation.

'Interestingly, Morton sells it as a true story passed to him by an agent and published as fiction, a literary ploy often used by master thriller writer Jack Higgins. Let's just say that it works better than Higgins.' – Danny Collins, author of *The Bloodiest Battles*

'...The best scenes are the one-on-one confrontations, claustrophobic closed room battles of expert second-guessing. One particular superb scene is beautifully choreographed and delivered, dragging the reader into the sweat-soaked reality of being stalked by a stronger killer...' – *Murder Mayhem & More*

Leon Cazador, P.I.

MISSION: TEHRAN

Tana Standish, Psychic Spy
in Iran, 1978

1978. Iran is in ferment and the British Intelligence Service wants Tana Standish's assessment. It appears that CIA agents are painting too rosy a picture, perhaps because they're colluding with the state torturers.

Allegiances and loyalties are strained as Tana's mission becomes deadly and personal. Old friends are snatched, tortured and killed by SAVAK, the Shah's secret police. She has to use all her skills as a secret agent and psychic to stay one step ahead of the oppressors and traitors.

As the country stumbles towards the Islamic Revolution, the Shah's grip on power weakens. There's real concern for the MI6 listening post near the Afghan border. Only Tana Standish is available to investigate; yet it's possible she could be walking into a trap, as the deadly female Spetsnaz fighter Aksakov has been sent to abduct Tana. Meanwhile, in Kazakhstan, the sympathetic Yakunin, the psychic spy tracking Tana, is being side-lined by a killer psychic, capable of weakening Tana at the critical moment in combat with Aksakov. Can Yakunin save Tana without being discovered?

In the troubled streets of Iran's ancient cities and amidst the frozen wastes on the Afghan border, Tana makes new friends and new enemies...

'... The locations are so finely drawn we can almost reach and touch them, the atmosphere so vivid that we can shut our eyes and sense ourselves there.'

Nik Morton

MISSION: KHYBER

Tana Standish, Psychic Spy
in Afghanistan, 1979-1980

In the aftermath of *Mission: Tehran*, psychic spy Tana Standish crossed into Afghanistan, accompanied by agent Alan Swann. Their rendezvous with Mike Clayton was delayed and while they waited for him in Herat, Tana befriends a Soviet forces family, intent on discovering details about the presence of General Pavlovsky. They're then caught in a devastating civil uprising....

Inexorably, the Soviets are being drawn into the politics of Afghanistan. And Clayton, Swann and Tana are linked with the heroic Massoud, the tyrant President Amin and the mujahedeen. Tana makes new friends and new enemies in her constant fight against injustice.

Professor Bublyk is still trying to locate Tana – and the missing Spetsnaz agent Aksakov. Distrustful of the psychic Yakunin, he recruits killer Klimov. Together, they imprison Yakunin in order to draw Tana out to rescue him.

Tana is aware that it must be a trap. But she owes her life to Yakunin, even though they have not met...

A tense cat-and-mouse battle of wits stretches the length and breadth of the country – to the far reaches of the Wakhan corridor, the Special Psychiatric Hospital in Dushanbe, Tajikistan, and ultimately to the Khyber Pass.

'... Morton doesn't skimp on lavish descriptions of the Afghan wilderness, the indigenous clans, their language, customs and heritage... If you read crime fiction to immerse yourself in a sense of place and time then *Mission: Khyber* will be perfect for you. Almost every chapter provides a potted history of a region and its people, from an archaeological perspective through to the religious upheavals which fuel unrest to this day. This is a spy story with a history lesson sneaked inside it.' – *Murder Mayhem & More.*

Leon Cazador, P.I.

CHILL OF THE SHADOW

In her search for truth she found love – with a vampire!

This cross-genre thriller is set in present-day Malta and has echoes from pre-history and also the eighteenth century Knights of Malta.

Malta may be an island of sun and sand, but there's a dark side to it too. It all started when some fishermen pulled a corpse out of the sea... Or maybe it was five years ago, in the cave of Ghar Dalam?

Spellman, an American black magician, has designs on a handpicked bunch of Maltese politicians, bending their will to his master's. A few sacrifices, that's all it takes. And he's helped by Zondadari, a rather nasty vampire.

Maltese-American investigative journalist Maria Caruana's in denial. She can't believe Count Zondadari is a vampire. She won't admit it. Such creatures don't exist, surely? She won't admit she's in love with him, either...

Detective Sergeant Attard doesn't like caves or anything remotely supernatural. Now he teams up with Maria to unravel the mysterious disappearance of young pregnant women. They're also helped by the priest, Father Joseph.

And there are caves, supernatural deaths and a haunting exorcism.

Just what every holiday island needs, really.

Where there is light, there is shadow…

'… a strong structure and is full of rich writing and action. The plot has page turning twists and the main characters are likeable, especially the female lead. I hadn't read a vampire book in a while and was reminded of how intensely gruesome they can be. While this one has its squeamish moments it's not atypical for the genre, and I can't help liking a well written book! The Malta setting was perfect, making this a great escape read.'

Nik Morton

THE BREAD OF TEARS

When she was a cop, she made their life hell.
Now she's a nun, God help them!

Before taking her vows, Sister Rose was Maggie Weaver, a Newcastle policewoman, who, while uncovering a serial killer, suffered severe trauma. While being nursed back to health she becomes a nun. In her new calling she finds herself sent to London to run a hostel for the homeless. Here, while doing good works, she combats prejudice and crime.

As she attempts to save a homeless woman from a local gang boss, events crystallise, taking her back to Newcastle, the scene of her nightmares, to play out the final confrontation against drug traffickers, murderers and old enemies in the police.

She finds her spiritual self and a new identity. She is healed through faith and forgiveness. It's also about her surviving trauma and grief – a triumph of the human spirit, of good over evil.

'This is a gritty and at times downright gruesome thriller. Written in the first person, Morton has achieved a true sense of feminine appeal in Maggie, the narrator, and despite her religious calling, she comes over as quite a sexy woman. Sister Rose (Maggie) is so cleverly well developed by the author that one could almost imagine that a female wrote the book. I found myself totally empathising with this full-blooded, gutsy woman and as such I was rooting for her all the way… All the characters and horrific events in this crime thriller are extremely visual and well-drawn, making this a riveting read. It would make a brilliant TV series!'
– Jan Warburton, author of *The Secret, A Face to Die For*

Leon Cazador, P.I.

AN EVIL TRADE

Tigers slaughtered to cure pimples!

Laura Reid likes her new job on Tenerife, teaching the Spanish twins Maria and Ricardo Chávez. She certainly doesn't want to get involved with Andrew Kirby and his pal, Jalbala Emcheta, who work for CITES, tracking down illegal traders in endangered species. Yet she's undeniably drawn to Andrew, which is complicated, as she's also attracted to Felipe, the brother of her widower host, Don Alonso.

Felipe's girlfriend Lola is jealous and Laura is forced to take sides – risking her own life – as she and Andrew uncover the criminal network that not only deals in the products from endangered species, but also thrives on people trafficking. The pair are aided by two Spanish lawmen, Lieutenant Vargas of the Guardia Civil and Ruben Salazar, *Inspector Jefe del Grupo de Homicidios de las Canarias*.

Very soon betrayal and mortal danger lurk in the shadows, along with the dark deeds of kidnapping and clandestine scuba diving....

'... Nik Morton has woven a masterfully written fictional story based on these appalling facts - a thriller and romance rolled into one that draws you in with plenty of suspense and fast paced action. Each chapter ends with a hook leading you eagerly on to the next. The characters and all the location settings on the island are colourfully realised.'

Also published by Manatee Books:

THE WELLS ARE DRY

Jennifer Morton

Art historian Ashley Bourne finds her emotions turned upside down as she seeks solace and forgetfulness in the pretty hill village of Pozos Secos where secrets and lies, mystery and danger abound. And the village wells keep drying up.

As she strives to solve the mystery of missing paintings and heirlooms, Ashley is torn between her deep feelings for financial wizard Tom Kerr and charismatic aristocrat, Francisco Romero. Is Fran the saint everyone believes him to be or a gentleman thief as Tom suspects?

Only after she has experienced the dangers of rogues, revolvers, fire, flood, wild boar and earth tremors, will she find the answers she has been seeking.

Sample Amazon reviews:

'A romantic mystery set in Southern Spain – a palette laden with colour and surprises!'

'An assault on the senses: the sights, sounds and smells and colours of Andalusia. And love…'

'I enjoyed this book enormously and it's certainly quite a page-turner… Mystery, conspiracy and deception abound… The storyline twists and turns… keeps you constantly guessing from chapter to chapter. Altogether, a fascinating recipe to keep you enthralled until the hugely dramatic denouement. The author's authentic knowledge of art and Spanish culture is colourful and well defined. I found her wonderfully, vivid descriptions of this part of Spain hugely evocative.'

Leon Cazador, P.I.

FLORESKAND: WINGS

Morton Faulkner

Floreskand, where myth, mystery and magic reign.

The sky above the city of Lornwater darkens as thousands of red tellars, the magnificent birds of the Overlord, wing their way towards Arisa.

Ulran discovers he must get to Arisa within seventy days and unlock the secret of the scheduled rites. He is joined in his quest by the ascetic Cobrora Fhord, who harbours a secret or two, and also the mighty warrior Courdour Alomar, who has his own reasons for going to Arisa. They learn more about each other – whether it's the strange link Ulran has with the red tellar Scalrin, the lost love of Alomar, or the superstitious heart of Cobrora.

Plagued by assassins, forces of nature and magic, they cross the plains of Floreskand, combat Baronculer hordes, scale snow-clad Sonalume Mountains and penetrate the dark heart of Arisa. Here they uncover truth, evil and find pain and death.

"A fast-paced fantasy adventure as an innkeeper, a city dweller full of surprises, and a long-lived warrior, join forces in a race against time. Their quest is to save the red tellars, the giant birds, which are the wings of the overlord. Along the way even the weather becomes a powerful adversary and the three are tested almost beyond endurance. Tensions and evocative language keep the reader turning the pages to the very end!"- Anne E. Summers, author of *The Singing Mountain*

An expansive and well thought story, a must-read for lovers of magic and military fantasy. - Kate Marie Collins, best-selling author of *Daughter of Hauk, Mark of the Successor* and *Son of Corse*

Nik Morton

FLORESKAND: KING

Morton Faulkner

When Ulran and Cobrora Fhord left Lornwater on their quest to resolve the mystery of the red tellars (*Floreskand: Wings*), the city was ripe for rebellion against King Saurosen, holder of the Black Sword.

In charge of the Red Tellar Inn, Ulran's son Ranell is drawn into a conspiracy with nobles to support Prince Haltese, the king's heir, to overthrow the tyrant. Inevitably, as a mining disaster and a murder in a holy fane stoke the fires of discontent, open rebellion swamps the streets.

Conflict turns into civil war, where the three cities' streets become a battleground. Conflict is not confined to Lornwater, however. There's fighting below ground in the mysterious tunnels and caves of the Underpeople, and within the forest that surrounds the city, and ultimately in the swamps and lakes of Taalland.

Subterfuge, betrayal, conspiracy, intrigue, greed, revenge and a thirst for power motivate rich and poor individuals, whether that's Lord Tanellor, Baron Laan, Gildmaster Olelsang, Lord-General Launette, ex-slave-girl Jan-re Osa, Captain Aurelan Crossis, Sergeant Bayuan Aco or miner Rujon.

Muddying the fight are not only bizarre creatures – the vicious garstigg, the ravenous lugarzos or the deadly flensigg – but also the mystics from the Sardan sect, Brother Clen, Sisters Hara, Illasa and Nostor Vata.

At stake is the Black Sword, the powerful symbol that entitles the holder to take the throne of Lornwater.

'... the world of Floreskand, a very cultivated creation.' - Nigel Robert Wilson, British Fantasy Society review of *Wings*

Printed in Poland
by Amazon Fulfillment
Poland Sp. z o.o., Wrocław